Kenner Deene

The Schoolmaster of Alton

Vol. II

SALZWASSER
VERLAG

Kenner Deene

The Schoolmaster of Alton

Vol. II

Reprint of the original, first published in 1863.

1st Edition 2022 | ISBN: 978-3-37500-277-0

Verlag (Publisher): Salzwasser Verlag GmbH, Zeilweg 44, 60439 Frankfurt, Deutschland
Vertretungsberechtigt (Authorized to represent): E. Roepke, Zeilweg 44, 60439 Frankfurt, Deutschland
Druck (Print): Books on Demand GmbH, In de Tarpen 42, 22848 Norderstedt, Deutschland

THE

SCHOOLMASTER OF ALTON.

A Tale.

IN THREE VOLUMES.

BY

KENNER DEENE,

AUTHOR OF

VOL. II.

London

1868.

THE SCHOOLMASTER OF ALTON.

CHAPTER I.

A WEDDING.

Ella dismissed her maid hastily and imperiously, she double locked her door, she partly undressed, and then, having stirred her fire into a blaze, and wrapped herself in a dressing gown, she paced up and down her room for hours; she could not bear the thought of lying down with all that tumult of anger and disappointment ringing in her ears and swelling at her heart—refused, absolutely refused by that monkey of a Challoner—and then the taunt of the monster came back to her mind, "you couldn't find another man in the world to marry you, just because you're so poor." She had thought him a fool for his pains at the time, and yet he had been in the right. "Wretch, wretch," and he would triumph over her, he would tell her again and again, that she might thank her stars that she had taken his fancy. He would glory in Challoner giving her up, and he would divine it too, he would discover it all at once, how he would chuckle and gloat over it; his loathsome kisses! Ellen seemed yet to feel them on her lips when she thought of him. "*Never*, *never*," muttered the girl, between her teeth. "I *never* will marry the monster; but I can't take a situation either, I could not be a tame toady like Miss Hall. Oh, dear me, what shall I do? what shall I do?" she wrung her hands, sat down before her fire and cried a little. "If I could go upon the stage, I should soon earn plenty of money, I have a taste for acting; but they say a girl is not respectable upon the stage, unless she's married; I wish I was married, then I would go about, and make my fortune somehow; if I could only get somebody to marry me to-morrow, I would do it, and make a bargain that they were never to seek me, or to find out who I was, and then I should be safe from the monster for ever." This wild idea having once entered her head, she actually began to turn it over in her mind as feasible; she had always been impressed with the idea that a young unmarried woman was never to go about alone, on her own responsibility, or that she would be irreparably lost; this was one o Mrs. Thorpe's notions, and it had grown up with Ella.

When Martin Cruize had given her that unflattering sketch of her characteristics he had been gifted with a sort of prescience and insight which probably sprang from his great love for her. It was true that she could endure nothing, and that though she liked her own will, she could be made to give it up if only she could be made to believe that it *was* her *own* will to do so. But in this case everybody had bullied her; the monster had scoffed, and spoken insultingly of making her his wife against her will; the darling had coolly washed his hands of her altogether, accompanying his rejection of her love with cold advice to marry the monster. Her parents had shown her only two alternatives, Poverty or Macnellan; both of these she dreaded and hated, neither of them would she endure. She would be a gay, brilliant actress, she would make her fortune on the stage, but she would enter there respectably; she would be a married woman, she would marry somebody, no matter who, but somebody who did not know her by name or sight, and whom she would never see again. She gave up all thought of love, henceforth and for ever, just because she was disappointed in the darling; she had fancied herself so much attached to him, and in her mad freak of fancy she settled it in her own mind that there was an end of love for ever for her, and that it was a thing which she was eminently qualified to do without both by nature and disposition. It was not until towards morning that this hair-brained, beautiful mad-cap retired to rest.

* * * *

The foggy frosty November day had just arisen, and the gaunt and worn schoolmaster of Alton had left his bed, and was groping his way down the narrow staircase. His frugal breakfast was laid out for him, early as it was, his half loaf, his piece of butter, his little black tea pot, his sugar basin, his milk jug with its broken spout. He called his landlady to bring him his kettle, and she brought it in and set it on the fire, where the newly lighted fagots crackled, and the lumps of coal looked black and cold as yet.

"How dark the mornings is, Mr. Cruize," said Mrs. King, giving the fire a poke.

"They are," says Martin gloomily.

"Here's your caddy, Mr. Cruize, when the kettle boils."

"Thank you."

"Mr. Cruize, I suppose you couldn't pay me the rest of the rent to-day? There's the other thirty shillings due yet."

"No, I can't," said Martin in a blustering voice. He was sadly out of temper, poor fellow; he had sent his mother three pounds a fortnight before, and he had never been able to get a farthing from Leslie or the instruction of the boys. As for Mr. Thorpe's bill, he had not sent that in at all.

"I wish you could soon," said Mrs. King. "I owe, you see, for my own rent, and it's so awkward; my 'usband, he's always aksing about that thirty shillings."

"Tell him to come in and ask me."

"It's very odd a young man can't pay his rent, and got his forty pound a year and other teaching besides," said Mrs. King, who was a civil woman enough when civilly spoken to, but somewhat of a vixen when saucily addressed.

"Yes, it's very odd—it's extremely odd," said Martin, speaking as though to himself. "Now, Mrs. King, will you walk out of my room?"

"I shall tell Mr. Yardly as I don't think you can be going on right," said the landlady in a high key. "You're quite changed from the civil spoken young man you was at one time. I shall tell him you're out late a night's, he's often arksed me if you was steady —see if I don't."

Martin hardly knew what she was saying in his abstracted wretched state, he often hardly knew what he was saying himself.

"Why the devil don't you leave the room?" he said fiercely.

She retired; calling out in a high key (for the benefit of her quiet husband above stairs, whose *arksing* after the rent was pure fiction), "See if I don't let Mr. Yardly know what sort of a swearing riotous fellow he's got in his school, see if I don't!"

When she was gone Martin sat down and sighed bitterly.

"Do I bully and swear at women? I shall copy that brute Leslie, and beat small children next, I suppose; and all because I love and am poor—poor as a pauper! I must do something soon, or I shall lose my reason."

While he sat buried in gloomy thoughts like these the fagots crackled more and more, the kettle began to sing, presently it boiled over. He took it off and set it on the hob, then he made his tea, cut himself some bread and butter, and began to eat and drink.

The fog cleared a little, the coals gathered heat, the food warmed him; he began to feel rather more cheerful, an atom more hopeful. He looked at his pinchbeck turnip, it was a quarter-past eight. Then came a tramping up the garden walk, it was the postman. He sprang to the door to avoid seeing Mrs. King again, he received in his hand a letter in a coloured envelope directed in his mother's writing; he opened it, read it, and five minutes later he was tearing wildly across the roads without his hat, in the direction of the curate's lodgings.

Hatless and ghastly, and with his hair in wild disorder, the schoolmaster stood in the presence of the curate, he held the open letter in his hand. The curate had risen from his breakfast table, and he answered the gaze of Martin with one of gentle inquiry.

"I want one hundred pounds before to-morrow night, said, Martin, I want a hundred pounds, I must have a hundred pounds, lend it me, Mr. Clyne, for God's sake, I will work my flesh off my bones until I have paid you again."

"Sit down, and tell me all about it."

"I can't, I never could, there, read that letter, it's from my mother; she is a forger, the man will let her off, if the money is returned by the day after to-morrow, read the note, read the note!"

The curate read the blurred, blotted writing executed in haste, and with the stump of the quill, and the clotted ink.

"Sit down, do pray sit down," was all the curate would say.

"Can't you get me the money? won't you give me your name to a bill? won't you help me?" asked Martin.

"Nobody would cash a bill on my acceptance. I have tried it before to help a friend. I should be years paying a sum like that if I lived, and I might die."

"Then, then, you can't help me; I waste my time here?"

"I will try to think of some plan; shall we go to Mr. Yardly?"

"I could not, I could not humble myself to him."

"*I* will take the letter, and lay the case before him; he is a wealthy man."

"And a stingy, hard, grasping one, he

would not give ten pounds to save my mother, or any body's mother from hanging; it would be disgrace, degradation. No, no," and Martin staggered to a chair, and gasped for breath. The curate handed him a glass of water, he drank some, and revived.

"There is Mr. Thorpe at home now, a rich man, and a kind one, they say. At least, they give away a good deal, and you have taught the son, have you not? Let us go to him?"

"Never!" roared Martin, "never, I tell you!"

"Then, have you no friends of your own?"

"I have an old uncle up in the north, stingy, and hard, but it is just possible he might save my mother from the hulks; she is his sister's child."

"Apply to him then, shall I write the letter for you?"

"He would burn the letter, and perhaps return no answer; I must go to him, but I have no money for the railway journey."

"I can lend you that, how much do you want?"

"I wish *you* would go too; my uncle has such respect for the church; he would listen with veneration to whatever you said."

"I will go, certainly. Go home now, my poor friend, and put on warm wrappings, for the cold is piercing, and I will follow you down to your lodgings; we will walk into St. Jude's, we shall be in time for the eleven o'clock train, and the exercise will warm us; but no, you look faint, I shall order a fly from the Inn."

* * * *

Cumberland hills are capped with snow, and across the open country the wintry wind drives piercingly, the small trees, so unlike their giant kindred of the midlands, are stripped and naked, the walls that divide the fields look bleak and barren, and then through the gorge of the hills, the great screeching engine rushes, panting, and spitting out fire and vapour, and the long whirring train freighted with its human load shoots past into the gathering gloom of the evening. On, on, on, with wild shriek, and clouds of smoke, and red fire flame, on, on, through the dark north country, awakening the echoes of the hills, and then leaving all silent as before. At last the train stops at a little out of the way station, and a few passengers descend; we will follow two with a knapsack between them, wrapped in travelling coats, and with caps upon their heads; these are the curate and the schoolmaster, they have to follow a lonely road, between the windings of a hill, the ground is white with frost, the sky is black and lowering, in the west there is a red light, which grows fainter and fainter, and at last dies away, and the two men are pacing along in darkness; soon, however, the stars awaken, and look out with their watchful eyes upon the travellers; and then over a high mountain on the left the bright half moon rises in resplendent lustre, and she floats along as she has floated any time these six thousand years, leaving a track of glory in her path, and looking down calmly on the "unruly wills and affections of sinful men." The light shone with ghostly lustre over the bleak country side, it shimmered upon the dark shelves of the hills, it rested here and there upon the fences and fields, it slept upon the freezing bosom of a deep pool, which lay on the right of the travellers; they made no remarks upon the weird beauty of the night, each was wrapped in his own thoughts, but those of the curate doubtless tended heavenward.

At last Martin spoke. "We must cross those fields, to the left, there is my uncle's house," and a few more yards brought them to the front of a little white two-storied house, with two small windows on each side the entrance, one above the other, making four in all, there was a wicket gate which Martin lifted, and then he and his companion passed in. Farm, and outbuildings stood to the left, and the little white house had a black square over the door, on which figures were cut, which stated that it had been built in the year 1784. Martin knocked at the door with his clenched fist, then a great dog in a stable began to bark furiously, and presently footsteps sounded inside the house, and then the drawing of a bolt, and the door moved back on its hinges, and there stood a little old withered man, on the hard lines of whose face the moon-beams fell placidly. He did not know, for a minute or so, who his visitors were, until Martin spoke.

"Uncle Jock, it is I—Martin."

"Eh, Martin, lad, is't thee come hame?"

"And this gentleman, uncle, is the clergyman at Alton. We have some very sad news."

"Eh!" with a long drawn accent on the interjective. "I haup you've not been getten into mischief, lad?"

"Not myself; but, uncle, let us come to the fire, for we are half perished with cold."

"It's cauld enow I worrant ye," said Uncle Jock, leading the way through a little entry, to a large flagged kitchen, which was called "the house;" there were blackened rafters across the roof, but no ceiling, an oak dresser well filled with plates and jugs of all sizes, some wooden chairs, a deal table in the recess of a diamond-paned window, which looked out into the garden, a loud old clock in a case of polished wood, which ticked away lustily, a wide chimney place and a red fire roaring up it cheerfully. Uncle Jock stood in its light (when he had placed chairs for his guests), with his hands in his old torn pockets; he wore the dress of a working man, although he had many and many a snug hundred pounds in the Bank at Carlisle. He was nearly seventy years old, and he was wizened and shrunken and thin. He had very much the cut of a miser about him, had Uncle Jock.

"What's amiss, lad, to bring thee t' hame so sudden?"

"My mother is in great trouble," said Martin, and then he began his tale of shame and pain, and when he faltered and broke down, the Curate helped him on; at last he ceased, and he waited to hear what Uncle Jock would say.

"I couldn't do't, lad, I couldn't do't; that lass, thy mother, has been naught but pain and throuble ever since she came to t' warld, and her mother befur was t' saame; her mother must needs run away when she wast little more ner a bairn, and join t' play actors; thn she must needs marry one like t' hersel, and they died, and left yer mother to shift for hersel; it's been a sad throuble to me, sad indeed."

"But if you will help her now, Mr. Tures, you will save her from a prison for life. You will, so to speak, have her blood on your head if you refuse. You know we have our duty plainly written for us in God's book, and I daresay you remember what it says there—"Lend to him that asketh of thee, and from him that would borrow of thee, turn not thou away."

"Naa, naa," said the old man, "t'good buke dose na mean that; if I lend, it must be on good security to him who will pay me again."

"But the Bible says, if one will have thy coat give him thy cloak also."

"Naa, naa, I don't tak it that waay at all; it's wrang in the translaution there, I am thinking. I have me twa daughters married, with bairns of their aune; I canna give away a haunder pound of theirs to saave a wicked woman like yer moother. I did t'best for this lad, I fed 'im, and kep 'im, and tauld 'im his dauty, and when he grew big I put him to t'training college, and maad a gentleman of 'im. Naa, naa, sir, I canna gie 'im a haunder pound to save yon lass."

Martin knew the obstinacy of old Uncle Jock. He signed to the curate that it was useless to press the matter further, and he even rose to leave.

"Sit daun, sit daun," said Uncle Jock, "till I get yer yer teas. Martin, lad, is't t'come hame, and waunt staay to taak a bite and a sup?"

"No, uncle," said Martin. "I think you very hard and cruel; I think you very wicked. Remember, she is your own flesh and blood."

"Flesh and blaud—flesh and blaud!" said Uncle Jock. "Naa, naa, lad, it's no near a kin—a sister's bairn that runs away and marris a play acter. A haunder pound is a haunder pound. I might pay away that much every week for yon lass, and she would not be content."

"Good night," said Martin, shortly. "Mr. Clyne, we waste time here."

And the Curate followed the schoolmaster out of the house, into the passage, through the farm yard, and out into the fields.

"We can only return to the village by the

station," said Martin, "and sleep at the inn to-night; to-morrow I must go up to London, and throw myself on the mercy of this John Farar."

"Better ask Mr. Thorpe to lend it," urged the Curate, "he would be almost certain to do it; he is not a stingy man."

"Never, never," said Martin violently, "if I cannot save my mother by other means than that, I will cut my throat."

"Mr. Thorpe must be well able to do it now," said the Curate, "his daughter is going to marry such a very rich man."

"What?" thundered the schoolmaster.

"Did you not know? why the wedding is to come off next week. Mr. Yardly told me last night; and with such an immensely wealthy man as that in the family, and the wedding festivities coming on, and besides being an open-handed man, it would be the very time to get a loan of the money. I would ask Miss Thorpe, if I were you."

"Would you?"

"Yes, she is such a free, generous girl, she would fly to do anybody a service. She would ask Mr. Macnellan himself for the money."

"Is that his name?"

"Yes."

Martin thought of the fair-faced darling, and supposed that he was the rich fiancée of Ella; the gossip of Mr. Yardly sunk on his heart like lead, and he thought much more of Ella than of his mother when he entered the village inn. The curate ordered tea and beds for two, and they sat down to a well supplied table in the inn parlour; but although Martin had tasted no food since the morning, he could touch nothing, he felt that any attempt to eat would choke him; the good Curate urged him in vain, and at last partook of his meal alone.

Soon afterwards he proposed retiring to rest, and Martin followed him mechanically to the landing where their little bedrooms stood,and there they parted, but the semblance of rest seemed a mockery to Martin, he never even attempted to undress, but paced his room wildly for some time, and at last descended to the inn parlour, where the embers of the fire still smouldered, and these he raked up again, and piled more fuel on, and then he sat down moodily before it, with his fingers clenched among his thick hair, and he remained abstracted and stirless for a time.

In the bar of the Golden Heart there were customers talking and smoking, and there was a jolly landlord with a red face and a bald head, who talked and smoked also. Then the clock struck ten, and the down train came screeching to the station, which lay near, and there it stopped a few moments, and then rushed off again. Presently a vehicle, which was accustomed to wait at the station, to convey any chance passengers to the nearest towns, or any of the seats of the gentry around, drove up to the door, and there descended from it a lady, young apparently, to judge from her figure; but her face was hidden in a thick veil. She walked straight into the bar and said, in a distinct, clear voice:—

"I will give one hundred pounds to anybody who will marry me to-morrow morning."

The first idea, of course, was, that this must be a lunatic; a few laughed, some looked grave, all stared.

"You must not think me mad," pursued the lady, "wild as this statement seems. My friends wish me to marry a man whom I detest. I have run away from home, and I must be married to save myself from scandal; but understand that I will not remove my veil from my face, nor must the person who marries me seek to know my family. And he must sign a paper, promising never to seek me nor to claim me while he lives. The moment the ceremony is over we must part for ever, but it must be a person in great need of money, anybody will do, a labourer, a clerk, a stone mason."

"I'm sorry to saay, mum, all yon's marrid men," said the landlord, nodding towards his customers; "happen *I* should do, but I've a wife in t' house, who mighten't think it right, but I'd be bonnie well plaused to suit you if it was not for that."

"I don't want any joking, jeering, or sauciness," said the lady; "I want a man who will marry me, take his hundred pounds and leave me at once."

Now the landlord had some slight acquaintance with Martin, albeit he knew him not by the name of Cruize, but by his mother's name of Woodby. He had recognised him on his entry with Mr. Clyne, the curate, and thinking he heard some one in the little parlour stirring the fire he went there.

Martin started when he heard a footstep.

"Happen, Misther Woodby, you might want a haunder pound?"

Martin turned round.

"Who told you that?"

"Nobody, but there's that for you if you like," and the landlord told him his wild but true story.

He had expected to hear him laugh; to his surprise Martin only said excitedly:

"It is the very thing I want, where is the woman?"

"In the bar."

"Well, I don't want to see her; just give me a pen, ink, and paper. I'll sign anything she likes, and as for not seeing her again it is all I desire; in fact, I never want to see her," and Martin with trembling hand drew out a paper to this effect.

"I, Martin Woodby, on the consideration of receiving a hundred pounds, do promise never to seek nor to speak to the woman I marry again. Signed, Martin Woodby, this 20th day of November, 18—."

And the landlord carried the paper into "the bar." The lady had retired into a far corner of the room and seated herself, her face was still muffled. The landlord walked up to her with a grin and gave her the paper; she put her veil up a little that she might read it.

"Who is this man?" she said to the landlord.

"He's a respectable young maan, his uncle's a faarmer here."

"Well, and how is the wedding to be managed? I should like it as early in the morning as possible. Is there a church near?"

"Why, yes, right up close to the street; and the parson, too, lives close, and keeps licences."

"It would be as well to go and tell him to be up early to-morrow to marry a couple; if you will go to him, I will pay you well for your trouble. And this Woodby, he is in earnest, he will not fail me?"

"Would yer like to see him?"

"No," said the lady, shrinking, "I wish he would cover up his face to-morrow; I don't want to see him at all. And now, can I go to a room for the night? Send your wife to me with some tea," and haughtily the queer lady walked out of the room, and a roar of coarse laughter followed her exit.

The landlady brought her tea upstairs, but she saw no more of her face than the people downstairs.

What tale the landlord told the parson is not known, but it is certain that nothing happened to prevent this strangest of strange weddings. At the earliest dawn of day the muffled lady descended from her room, and followed by a few villagers, whom intense curiosity impelled, she entered the church, which was dimly lighted. The surpliced clergyman, whose fees were paid, stood book in hand behind the altar rails, and the bowed form of the schoolmaster, who sedulously turned his face away (according to the wishes of his bride), was on the steps. She never looked at him once, and then the exhortation began.

The clergyman had not at all an impressive

manner or voice, and thus it happened that neither of the strange beings who met under these wildly unnatural circumstances felt much more than weariness, and a great impatience for the ending of the ceremony. But when the words were spoken, "and therefore are not by any to be enterprised, nor taken in hand lightly, unadvisedly, or wantonly," it may be supposed that one at least felt some qualms of conscience. She gave no signs, however, and the ceremony proceeded, looked upon by both as a mere farce. Then the pastor turned to Martin, and asked him "If he would have that woman to be his wedded wife, to live together after God's ordinance in the holy estate of matrimony, to love her, to comfort her, honour and keep her, in sickness and in health, and forsaking all others keep him only unto her so long as they both should live."

And Martin said "I will," when he meant to leave her the next hour, and never see her face again.

Then the priest put the same question to the veiled woman, and when his gruff voice ceased, her silvery one pronounced the words,

"I will."

At that sound the schoolmaster started—almost bounded from the altar steps; the next moment his strong will conquered, and he stood still like a block of stone. WHO had promised before the altar of God, before those railings, where the sacred cup was passed, and the type of the bread of life eaten; who had promised to cling to him in sickness and in health, to *forsake* all others, and so keep only unto him? His next thought was that it must be the wild dream of a disordered fancy, an overtasked brain, this veiled woman on the altar steps, who had entered a poor inn, and publicly offered herself in marriage to anybody; this woman, who had probably some dark secret of her own to smother under the name of wife, this woman for whose unwomanly act he felt loathing, and contempt, and whom he would not have met there, unless he had first seen the money paid into the hands of the landlord——

Could this creature be Ella Thorpe, the gay, the pure, the proud, the light of her house, the idol of her circle? Was he not mad? Then he had to take her hand; did he recognise the slender fingers, which two weeks before he had held in his in the lumber room? Yes, yes, there was a plain gold signet on the fore finger, which he had noticed then, but if he had wanted more proof it was afforded when following the words of the priest, she again promised "to have and to hold *him*, from that day forth," again that voice. How did the ceremony end? In the dim light of the morning, they entered the vestry, and the names were entered in the book. "Ella Raikes, aged nineteen," "Martin Woodby, aged twenty-three," and she had never raised her eyes once to his face, that veiled, elfish creature. She had married, she knew not what, she cared not what, while he,—oh, what failed him now that he did not fold her tightly to his heart, and calling her *wife*, swear by all the waters above and below the earth that she should never leave him? But his promise, his mother, the money to save her!! Yes, that stain on his name, must not be allowed. She is gone, then, and whither? Will he see her again? will a time come when he can fulfil the vow he uttered on the chase? will he yet hold her to his heart, press his lips to hers, and call forth answering love from her? What is the wild tumult which fills his ears, which thumps at his heart, which thrills in his veins? is it mad joy, or only disappointed hope?

CHAPTER II.

"TO E. T."

Two days later a beautiful young lady, who called herself Mrs. Woodby, appeared rather late at the breakfast table, in a boarding house at Kensington, where she had taken up her residence the day before; the young gentlemen all admired her rapturously, even the ladies thought her charming. She had openly told them that it was her intention to seek an engagement on the stage; two or three offered her a chair, she took one with a sweet smile, and then carefully turned over the day's *Times*, and her eyes fell on these words:

"To E. T.—Return, return to your home; all cause of annoyance is for ever over. M. lies at the point of death."

She put the paper down, made a hasty excuse, and hurried to her room

"What had she done? what had she done?"

All right again at home, and she wife to a labourer, for so she fancied him, who perhaps might find her out some day. She sank on her knees and wept, then she rose and resolved not to care; the man never *could* know her again, by the dim lamp light and with her veil down. She had no idea of what he was like. No, she would go home, and be merry Ella Thorpe again. She would ride back Black Fan, fill the house with visitors, *take Latin lessons.* Yes, "E. T." would go home again, and "E. T." went.

CHAPTER III.

AT THE POINT OF DEATH.

WHO has lain *there*, and can recal the time without a shrinking and awe? Not so much felt at the moment, perhaps, as afterwards, because one is seldom fully conscious of one's danger at the time. But to have been *near*—close upon the immensity of eternity, with earth and its joys and sorrows fading into nothingness, and the great gates of a never-ending future opening on one's view, unsolvable, unsoluble, that with these gates always standing open to our hearthstones, at our bedsides, in our walks and drives, and travels, with friends and acquaintances entering into them on every hand, and with a *dead*, moral *certainty*, that we *must* enter them one day, we yet can live so lightly, so carelessly putting thoughts of death into the far distance, when our hair shall be whitened, and our eyes dimmed.

It must, I suppose, be a merciful provision of the "All Merciful," for with a constant thought of death the spirit would become heavy and sad. I cannot, I do not believe those good people who tell us that we ought to live with the continual idea of departure in our minds. I believe God *must mean us to forget it* while we are in health. If there is any other evil in our future, if we dread to lose the good opinion of a friend, if there is an uncertain law suit pending, or a house the lease of which will expire in five years and we be minus the rent which now comes in pleasantly, we fret and lie awake, and scheme how we may best ward off the impending evil or loss; whereas about the great mysterious change which is to last *for ever*, and about which we have all heard stories and surmises horrible enough to freeze the marrow in our bones, we seldom scheme or think at all. It must be *the will of* GOD that we should not distrust Him, but with full and perfect faith in that munificent goodness which filleth the earth with food, and in that tender watchfulness which careth for the fall of the sparrows, we should leave all to Him who is greater than our fears, and who will in the bosom of the Unseen be as truly our protector as he has been here. If it were not so, He would not have made this earth so green and pleasant—He would not have carpeted it with flowers and filled it with the poetry of nature. I hope I am writing nothing wrong, but I only state my own simple convictions.

Macnellan lay at the point of death. On the morning when Ella was missed he had accompanied Mr. Thorpe to St. Jude's, hoping to find a trace of her, and imprudently crossing the rails when the train was in sight he had slipped, and the engine was upon him before he had time to recover himself. There was help at hand, so that his life had been spared, but a leg and an arm were completely severed from his body. He now lay ill at Alton Hall, whither he had been removed so ill that the doctors despaired of his life. He was wracked with fever, which mounted to his brain, and he lay in anguish, wildly howling out the name of Ella, and threatening to ruin Mr. Thorpe if she was not brought to his presence.

Mrs. Thorpe, with inimitable tact, contrived to persuade the attendants and doctors that the whole of Macnellan's ravings had no foundation. Then she never showed the least anxiety about her daughter, but told the servants she had only gone to visit Miss Jesson in London (she knew no Miss Jesson), and then she put the advertisement to E. T. in the *Times* and the *Daily Telegraph*, and it happened as she desired.

On the evening of the fifth day from her

departure, Ella returned, looking fagged and rather pale, but not out of spirits; she came in a fly from St. Jude's; and she said, as she embraced her mother,

"You see what a determined prickle I am, dear Mater. I've been to London, and I would go again if the poor old boy recovered and became troublesome."

Mrs. Thorpe kissed the girl coldly.

"I cannot approve of your conduct," she said; "fortunately you have a prudent mother, or your character would be damaged for life; a young unmarried woman should never travel alone, and where did you stop in London?"

"At a boarding house in Kensington; a very nice boarding house. I found it by an advertisement, lots of respectable people there."

"And did you give your real name?"

"I said I was married, a Mrs. Woodby," said Ella, colouring.

"That was wise, at least, it made you respectable in the eyes of the people; but, Ella, what persuaded you to behave in such an unlady-like wild manner. Nobody forced you to marry Macnellan; you know you were at liberty to refuse him at once."

"But, dearest mother, what a life I should have had, living in poverty in some dull London street, and with your reproachful eyes, and papa's, and Arthur's too always upon me."

"What then was your wise intention?"

"Ah! mamma, the poor old monster may not mean to turf after all, and if he gets well, you may all want me to marry him, and then if I let out the secret, you may prevent me from flying again to my refuge."

"Poor Macnellan will never trouble us again, Ella."

"Don't hollo, until you are out of the wood, mater mine. Can I have something to eat?"

"Certainly."

And Ella had some luncheon, then she went and brushed her hair, and changed her dress; she had taken very few clothes with her, on her wild escapade, and then her father came, and told her she *must* come and see Macnellan.

All the visitors were gone, the servants went about the house in list slippers, and with hushed voices; it seemed a mournful changed house. Across the richly carpeted passages, and into a darkened room, where a wicked and ugly sinner lay "at the point of death," it was a terrible sight, that man with his features naturally repulsive, distorted to ghastliness, his head close shaven, his green eyes starting from their sockets. Mr. Molson, an eminent physician from St. Jude's, stood by the bed side with a grave serene face; he signed to Ella to be noiseless, and to approach the bed; the thoughtless creature paused appalled. Macnellan knew her at once, and attempted to spring towards her, but the scalding pain in his dissevered limbs caused him to sink back, with an expression of rage and anguish.

"You are come then, beautiful she-devil; do you think to escape me? I will have a parson to the bed-side, and he shall marry us, or I will sell up your father's house;" he ended by giving utterance to a frightful oath. "Come here, come close." Ella shrunk back. "Come close, you fiend! it is through you I suffer all this, come close."

It was not a loathing of an expected embrace that kept Ella back, it was because she read a devilish intent in the eye of the maniac, she thought that he would at least bite out a piece of her flesh if she ventured near him. Mr. Molson came round her, and whispered—

"Soothe him, say something kind."

One always obeys a physician in a sick room. Ella said, hastily, "Mr. Macnellan, don't be angry with me; you know I could not help your accident, you will be well soon, if you lie still, and I shall come in every day, and see how you get on."

He was softened for a moment by her gentleness.

"And you will marry me, Ella?"

"Oh! yes, of course, when you are well," said Ella, blushing at her own lie.

"You ought to marry me now?"

"You are not strong enough to bear the ceremony; you will be soon well."

"*Liar!*" roared Macnellan, as a new spasm of agony distorted his countenance. "You know well I am dying, dying, going down fast, down, down to hell, to everlasting burnings, and you rejoice, fiend, she wolf, adulteress!"

Ella started violently at that last unjust epithet.

"You would be, if I married you, you know you would. You will be yet if I do marry you; you look like one; where is your doll-faced favourite?" and he added words of coarse abuse, and vile accusation, which sent Ella weeping violently from the room.

Doctor Molson never heeded his ravings, and he even followed Ella to administer sal-volatile, and to entreat her not to distress herself.

Later in the day when Ella sat alone with her mother in the breakfast-room by the fire, she asked what the visitors had thought of her absence, and when they had left?

"Oh! I said you had gone to visit a friend; of course, I was obliged to say to Challoner that it was to avoid Macnellan, you had gone for I found he knew all about it."

"What did he say?" asked Ella, turning crimson.

"Very little; he seemed sorry, said you would be certain to alter your mind, and return; and then he packed up his things, and went off, before Macnellan and your father started; they were going to London," (Ella could scarcely repress a smile at the mistake), "and the Kilrudereys and the Elliots went off in a body, on the return of Macnellan after his accident—Holmes and Rollins left, you know, a fortnight since."

"And what did the ladies think of me?"

"They knew nothing whatever—they may have surmised—they found me cheerful and calm outwardly."

"Good mamma," and Ella kissed her mother.

CHAPTER IV.

A NEW SPOKE IN THE WHEEL.

CHALLONER had been gone a week, winter had spread over the land, the water froze, and the snow fell, and the wind howled, and the Leslies were very poor. Mr. Leslie had, long ago, spent the two twenty pound notes which he had brought down in September, he had been to London since, and had returned with another instalment, and that was gone too, and debts were dreadfully pressing, and nobody would trust, and even the landlord, who had been paid a good part of his bill, began to look glum. Pauline sat desolate by the fire, on a low seat, reading one of George Sand's most equivocal novels in the original; she had fretted a great deal about Hubert, she was positive he loved her, she only needed money. Leslie was sitting in an arm chair, at the other side of the fire. Mrs. Leslie was absent, engaged in some household work.

"Oh dear me!" said Pauline, with a yawning sigh, throwing the book down.

"Tired?"

"Of my life here. Oh, I can't stand it any longer!"

"Neither shall you—I have a charming scheme in hand, but you must let me form my plot while these wreaths of smoke float out of the tube of my pipe, like any German metaphysician, or plotting romancer working out 'a strange story.' I mean you to have plenty of money, Pauline, before three months are over, enough to tempt your lover into marriage, if he cares truly for you; but what a casting of pearls before swine!!"

"Papa?"

"Yes, my dove of doves, who is then worthy of you?"

"Only Pappalie."

"Well, if I hadn't married Mrs. Leslie when you—"

Just then Mrs. Leslie came in. She walked up to Leslie, and put a bill into his hand.

"Three pounds ten shillings for boots," he tossed it in the fire. "Confound you! why do you bring it here?"

"That's just what she likes," said Pauline, "she is in her glory now."

"Mrs. Crane has been asking for the rent again."

"Let her ask, and be d——d to her," said Leslie, and Pauline burst out laughing.

"Pauline, darling, why don't you wear your nice purple merino, trimmed with velvet, this cold weather?"

"I'm saving it for London, Pappalie—it is so beautifully made, and there is nobody to see us in this beastly hole."

"True, but I hate to see you in that washed out thing, my pet isn't so neat as she was."

Leslie himself was the perfection of neatness.

"Can't you manage to take me somewhere next week, Papa? I shall positively become insane if I stay here any longer."

"We will see, sweet one." Just then Leslie raised his eyes with a scowl. "Here's that confounded fellow the schoolmaster come after his bill again;" then to his wife, "Go and say I'm out!"

"I am tired of saying that."

"You are—go at once;" and Mrs. Leslie went and opened the door to Martin Cruize.

The schoolmaster raised his cap.

"Might I speak to Mr. Leslie?"

"You are come about your bill, Mr. Cruize?"

"Yes!"

"Mr. Leslie cannot pay it just yet."

Martin looked down gloomily.

"It is very inconvenient to me to wait any

longer, Mrs. Leslie; in fact, I am pestered myself for money, do you think Mr. Leslie can manage it by next week?"

"I don't know, but, Mr. Cruize, you shall not lose it, I promise you. I will take care that, the next time Mr. Leslie receives an instalment, you are paid." She was grateful for his gentleness and his pains taking with her children.

Martin said, "Thank you," raised his cap again and turned from the door; and now he was pacing the frost bound lane with abstracted eyes and unquiet mien. He had reached London time enough to save his mother with his strangely earned money, and the affair was hushed up, and no breath of suspicion attached itself to her.

The curate, who did not awaken until after the ceremony, was kept in complete ignorance o the affair, for Martin had told the landlord not to reveal it to him; and thus, though all the parish of Yanston, in Cumberland, knew of young Martin Woodby's strange wedding, no shadow of suspicion could possibly reach to Ella Thorpe, of Alton, two hundred miles south, and the only being on earth who knew her secret, *knowing her* to be the step daughter of Mr. Thorpe, of St. Jude's County, was Martin Woodby, *her husband!*

And how did this husband, who madly adored his wife, mean to act? He was in blind ignorance of the real motives which had impelled her to her strange deed of the week past, he knew not where he stood, or what abyss might be yawning at his feet; he had wild ideas of winning wealth or fame somehow, and of then coming boldly forward to claim his wife, but how was he to begin?

He had returned to Alton the day before Ella; the absence of the Curate at the same time had disarmed all injurious suspicions on the part of Mr. Yardly, to whom he stated that the illness of one of his family had been the cause of his sudden journey, and to the Curate he had said that an old friend who had accidentally entered the Inn had advanced him the money; thus Martin had told untruths to each of these men, and he felt degraded in consequence, but what could he have done? he asked himself. A nice beginning for a man who wished to raise himself to the level of the wife he had married—to inaugurate himself as an unblushing liar; he was in debt too, he had helped his mother to his last shilling. *She* had nothing now save the produce of the silks and velvets bought in Regent Street, which on her release she had proceeded to sell; she might live on that for a time, and then Martin must again help her out of his salary. His landlady was impatient, and he owed for his boots;—a certain feeling forbade his asking for money at Thorpe's, and until he did so he knew he should not be paid. The Leslies might not pay him for months, and he had forestalled his quarter's allowance in consequence of his mother's demand, and already Mr. Yardly looked severely at him. What was he to do? so wretchedly poor, in debt, in a position where he could never rise?

If he were to go abroad? but no, Ella was at Alton, he had discovered that, that morning, and he could not tear himself from her presence. He had hardly expected to find her returning there, and he had made up his mind to seek her and follow her wherever she went, and now he ought to have been ravished to find her again at Alton, where he could see her nearly every day, even speak to her, but a sense of his poor, almost degraded position oppressed him; he had not felt it before the marriage; then, with a strong republican feeling, and a confidence in his powers, he had dared to call himself the equal of Ella even to her face; but now it was different, he was married to her, her money had saved his mother from the hulks, and he, a poor starving wretch, in debt for his boots!! could he dare to call her wife? ought he not rather to hide his head for ever from her, to pass out of her life, to leave her in peace, in plenty, among the refinements and elegancies of her home? but could he do it? was it possible to the schoolmaster, who had registered his vow in his deepest soul, who loved Ella as man seldom loves,—was it possible for him to sacrifice his great passion to considerations like these? No, ten thousand times no!! again and again he swore that he would make his wife love him, respect him, cling to him. Yes, though it should take years first, and though it should as it were cost him the coining of his heart's blood into money to purchase for her the comforts and the luxuries which were so necessary to her.

Martin went into his lodgings and partook of a frugal scanty meal, afterwards he went to his schoolroom, and patiently informed his pupils that London was the capital of England, and that two and three make five.

* * * *

Macnellan still lay in great danger on his

bed. Mr. Thorpe watched the changes in him anxiously, so did his wife; what end did these people desire to this illness? It would be superfluous to state that both would have been rejoiced to have seen Macnellan "safely landed on the other side of Jordan," as Ella impiously remarked, and Mr. Thorpe answered ill-humouredly enough—

"I care nothing about where he lands, but I should be glad to see the last of him."

Was this unnatural for selfish and worldly people, who owed the dying nearly the whole of their earthly goods, and who found in him an insulting creditor? they saw plainly enough that their beautiful girl would always shrink from the idea of marrying him, and they owned to each other that it *would* be a dreadful sacrifice. They dreaded besides that should he linger sufficiently long, the man would call his executors together, and pass the debt over to his next heir; no, the sooner he died the better, but still they gave him the best attention possible, and called in the assistance of Dr. Molson, a really clever person; they did not mean to kill him, they knew that such a proceeding would have been highly dangerous, and that even *neglect* might subject them to reproof, for it was by this time pretty well spread about that they owed the sick man large monies, and therefore they took all possible pains to care for him, and told only their dark wishes to each other, and wishes harm nobody; very few people under their circumstances would *not* have have wished the man dead. Only those who have an immense value for human life in the abstract, and who in the case even of a man, wicked and dangerous as poor Macnellan, would have shrunk from wishing him dead, as a great crime. There is no concealing the fact then, the Thorpes wished Macnellan to die, with their whole hearts, and there they stopped; neither of them would have accelerated his end by the raising of a finger, at the time of which I write, but when once a wicked or a selfish wish has taken root in the human heart, who can say what it may grow to?

Aye, poor, tortured, wicked "Crœsus," groaning with pain, thou had'st no pitying eye, no gentle voices round thy couch, none to whom thy loss would have been a gap in their circle; thou art in danger, Macnellan, on thy down bed in Thorpe's mansion; should the fiend temptation arise and point the way to freedom and release, leading safely and easily through the door of death to be entered by *thee* alone, I would not put much price upon thy chance of safety.

Ella was too young and light-hearted, too good-natured, and ignorant of evil, to enter into these feelings; she hardly believed in death, he had never crossed her path, she was simply glad that Macnellan had it not in his power now to injure her father, or to turn her out of her home, but she felt sorry for his sufferings; it would be a mercy for himself, she thought, if he could die, but still if he did recover, why something would be sure "to turn up" to benefit her father, and meanwhile, of course, they must take great care of the poor monster, and precious dull it was too, having such a patient in the house cutting off all her pleasures, and even preventing her from leaving home on a visit. And what a patient he was, raving incessantly in the delirium of fever, of wrongs, and sins, long ago committed, of unholy lusts, of dead paramours, of a long course of uncleanness, and vice, which made it unseemly for one young and innocent as Ella to remain within ear shot; he spoke sometimes regretfully of a dead wife, and a son drowned in his infancy; on this last theme, the old sinner would linger, almost tenderly; it seemed the one trait in his character which connected him to the human species, and redeemed him from the total alliance with animals, or with fiends.

"If that child had lived," said Macnellan, "he would have been a man now; he was my own lawful son, and I had much love for him, he should have been the heir to my fortune.

Hah, hah, he would have been young, and perhaps comely too, if he had lived, then this little black-eyed demon would not have despised him, not a young man," and again the monster used language which sent even Mrs. Thorpe, calm stoic as she was, blushing from the room. It was horrible to have a polluted old sinner with no reason left to guide him, letting out all the filthy fancies of his brain, and shocking a gentleman's household with expressions which made the hardest blush; it was detestable, it was *unbearable.* Nay, but it had to be borne.

If only something could be devised to restore his shattered reason; the doctor was afraid of too many sleeping draughts, and he was not given to the use of chloroform.

It was unbearable. Two days more of horrible ravings, of unmitigated anguish, but still the patient was alive; he was possessed of immense vitality, there seemed less than ever, a chance of a "happy release," and on the third day there came so deep a fall of snow, it was near the middle of December now, that footsteps fell quite noiselessly round the front of the house, and though the sun peeped out with a shy and sickly smile, nobody from Alton Hall ventured from the door step.

There came a ring at the great front bell, the footman went to the door, and there stood on the mat a rather stout florid, smiling gentleman; the footman knew him at once, he had often seen Mr. Leslie at church.

"Mr. Thorpe in?"

"There is a gentleman very ill in the house, sir, and no visitors are admitted, except the clergyman, and the doctors."

"Quite so," said Leslie, pleasantly, "but it is in regard to that gentleman that I wish to speak to Mr. Thorpe; just take him in that card, Mr. James Leslie, of Woodly; he has heard my name often, tell him I come at the instance of Mr. Yardly."

The footman then showed Mr. Leslie into

a little breakfast parlour, and went at once to his master, and he soon returned to tell Mr. Leslie to follow him to the library, a large luxurious room, in the Elizabethan style, where Mr. Thorpe was standing upon the rich rug before a splendid fire; he was a very haughty man, and stood a great deal upon his own position, he had heard of Leslie simply as a *nobody*, living at Woodly; he felt a little vexed too at the intrusion, he gave a very slight nod to his visitor, and motioned him coldly to a chair. Mr. Leslie was not the least abashed.

"I have in the first place to apologise for this intrusion."

"Not at all," but still Mr. Thorpe looked annoyed, and haughty.

"But I am one who like to render what service I can to my fellow creatures; in fact, I think it is the duty of every body to help those with whom they come in contact, if possible; it is solely with this idea, that I have called upon you, Mr. Thorpe, although I have lived nearly twelve months in your neighbourhood, and we are as yet quite unacquainted."

Mr. Thorpe felt a little uncomfortable at the implied reproach, as Mr. Leslie intended that he should; *he* had always felt vexed that the retired merchant should have neglected him, and his family, although as he had come completely unknown into the place, according to the usages of polite and conventional life, he ought to have reckoned upon being totally ignored by the county people, as he had been. But these same usages of conventional life are wounding instruments to many insignificant folks, who think themselves "as good as any body else," but cannot get great people to agree with them in that opinion.

"I did not know you had resided so long here, how do you like Woodly?" asked Mr. Thorpe, in a most refined and musical voice.

"Oh, immensely, I only came here for rest, retirement, a little fishing, and so on, but,

Mr. Thorpe, Mr. Yardly, with whom I am very well acquainted, informed me last night that you have a friend very ill in your house?"

"Yes."

"And that his delirium almost takes the form of insanity, so that your family are annoyed by the terrible nonsense he talks, and that is extremely disagreeable."

"Mr. Yardly is famed for repeating whatever he hears," said Mr. Thorpe, with heightened colour; "women and priests have little else to do but gossip."

Leslie laughed pleasantly; "Just so; but supposing it to be true, I have a speedy, safe way to remove the annoyance; I have learned it abroad."

"Ah!" in a polite tone of forbearance.

"Allow me to come here once or twice a day, I would undertake to soothe and pacify Mr.—— your friend, and to accelerate his recovery."

"Thank you; but we have the attendance

of Mr. Molson, in whom we feel great confidence."

"Exactly so; but he perhaps is not an advocate of mesmerism?"

"Mesmerism?"

"Yes; you see it would not interfere with his medicine or attendance; and all I shall ask is to be permitted to look at your patient, and make a few passes, and all his fury and ravings will cease."

"That would be a comfort, indeed," said Thorpe.

"Well, I am quite at your service; and I am perfectly confident of what I profess."

Mr. Thorpe felt a desire to shut up Macnellan's wicked mouth, but he felt no desire to have his private affairs canvassed more than they were already in the neighbourhood; and as yet little was distinctly known, only one or two confidential servants had been admitted into the old maniac's sick room; the honour of Dr. Molson was of course far beyond the faintest shadow of suspicion, and now if he admitted this interfering "nobody," what tales might not be carried abroad? and so Mr. Thorpe thinking the remedy worse than the evil, refused at once, politely, but firmly, to accept Mr. Leslie's services.

"I regret it very much," said Leslie, rising to go, "because I feel sure I could at once allay that fever of the brain, and with rest and quiet, your friend would perhaps recover, and if not, it would be but charitable to soothe his last moments."

"I would not for one moment think of taking such a responsibility on myself," was Thorpe's excuse; "at the same time, I am much obliged for your kindness;" and so the new *spoke* was not put into the *wheel* that morning, and Leslie went out feeling extremely disappointed; the plot which he had been forming the other day, when the wreaths of smoke had floated out of his pipe, seemed likely to fall to the ground.

o o o o o

"I'll tell you what, Doctor, that villain with the pink face and fine nostril—that rascal with the white hands and diamond ring, is worse than I am, old sinner as I look. I knew him in his youth—he was a libertine; but sly, sly, sly; no more heart than a rotten apple; cold and cautious; hah, hah, always greedy of gain. I had him under my thumb always; a woman loved him, and I made him leave her, just by throwing out a hint of a rich marriage; he nearly drove her mad—what did he care? I did it—I did it; but then, I tell you, I was baulked—baulked as I have been now, about his wanton step-daughter. He is a beggar, that man; he has reason to tremble at me. He thinks I shall die, hah, hah. Can't I make over his debt—won't I do it, if I live till next week? and his girl (whisper low, Doctor, and I'll tell you what) *she* is" here came words too polluted to be written; "and when I die, how will Thorpe live? That girl is beautiful, but not chaste, and Thorpe and his stick of a wife will sell her, ha, ha, without compunction; she shall be dragged down to the lowest depths of all that is degrading, and then she shall come to me —ha! ha! she shall come to me in hell, at last."

* * * * *

Mr. Thorpe stood pale, in the servant's hall; it was nine o'clock in the evening.

"Wilson," said he, to the footman, "put on your coat, and take a lantern, and cross the fields to Woodly, and call at Crane's, the farmer's—you know Crane's?—and ask, and beg Mr. Leslie, who is lodging there, to come down here at once, if he possibly can." Within an hour and a half from that time, Mr. Leslie entered Alton Hall, the doctor had just left, and he was shown into the library again; and that night he first put his *spoke* into the *Thorpe's wheel.*

CHAPTER V.

KATE HALL.

We have not forgotten Kate Hall, although we have not spoken of her for a long time. But amid the contending passions and strange circumstances which we have attempted to portray, we have not really lost sight once of the sweet pale face, and the sad-coloured gown, all through the secret dread caused by Ella's departure, all through the ravings of the unhappy patient, the rustle of her dress was still about the corridors, or her light step upon the wide stair-case; she was there silent, watchful, making herself useful preparing broth and jellies for the sick man;

carrying these to the door of his room, and then retiring having heard nothing, and not desiring to hear; woman's instinct, fine, subtle, tender, told her that the family were in trouble, that even upon the dashing Ella's face there was a slight cloud, and, on the evening when Mr. Leslie called to mesmerise Macnellan, happening to enter the little breakfast parlour to stir up the fire and see that all was in order, she found that young lady on a low footstool sobbing by the fireplace, and not attempting to conceal her sobs either. To offer sympathy where it is not asked is an unthankful office, but still Ella almost seemed to claim some pity, her *abandon* was so complete.

"Are you not well, Miss Ella?"

"Well enough, but miserable; oh, dear me!"

"Perhaps this gentleman may do Mr. Macnellan good, and then——"

"I'm sure I hope he won't. I wish the old sinner to turf it."

Catherine was by this time well enough used to Miss Ella's vocabulary to comprehend the meaning of her words.

"But, Miss Ella, that is a dreadful wish—death is terrible to us all—and for a man not in his proper mind, to pass out of life in dread, and in darkness, it is horrible!"

"Oh, yes, to you, with your evangelical notions, and your belief in pitch and brimstone. You should talk to Mr. Yardly, and then both of you could groan over 'the poor lost sinner,' together."

To hear solemn subjects treated lightly, mockingly, by a young and fair woman, is nearly always revolting. Let who will believe, or not believe in the dreadful reality of eternal punishment; let those who have a firm and unswerving faith in the God of the widow and the fatherless—in Him who heareth the young ravens when they cry—and "who sent His only begotten Son to die, that we might live." Let them who believe in this God, and who strive, as far as in them lies, to live in the light of his countenance, doing Him true and laudable service, and obeying his laws as best they may, let them believe or not believe in the eternity of the Divine wrath, in the implacability of Divine justice; and if they cannot reconcile the endless torture of millions, with the accepted propitiation for our sins, which was offered on Calvary, then let them enjoy their own opinions in peace—it can do them no hurt; but let them not mock at things connected with the awfulness of the unseen.

Ella, however, had never troubled her pretty head about these things, *nothing* was solemn to her; she who had stood on the altar steps, and plighted her troth to whom she knew not and cared not.

"My dear Miss Ella," said Catherine, who knew that further remonstrance would be thrown away on the volatile creature, "I am sorry to see you so distressed, but I will go away if you would rather be left alone, or shall I bring my work here?"

"What work are you doing?" asked Ella, raising her head with a sudden and frivolous interest in Catherine's words.

"I was trimming that white silk evening dress of yours."

"With pink satin rosettes down the front?" asked Ella.

"Yes."

"Oh, bring it to me; I should like to see it."

So Kate brought it in, and for nearly half-an-hour nothing was talked about but trimmings; then while Kate sewed, Ella relapsed into moody silence.

"I wonder," said she, at length, "if that mesmeriser will do the monster any good. I say, Catherine Hall, if he did get well and wanted me to marry him, I'd run away again."

"Ella!"

"I did run away; did you know that?"

"Not exactly. At least——"

"At least," said Ella, mocking her tone,

"don't talk balderdash! don't I know that you and all the servants know it quite well."

Ella was in a thorough bad humour.

"You and all the servants!"

Poor Kate Hall! it was too bad; she bent her head lower over her work, and just put her handkerchief to her eyes.

"Are you going to pipe your eye, too? we shall be a nice pair;" and then she laughed more good temperedly, and she moved her low seat right in front of the fire, and there she sat, her arms embracing her knees, her thick black hair escaping from its pins, and floating down her shoulders; her cheeks were crimson, her eyes were dancing with light, a tear or two still shone in them, and trembled on her long lashes, but still she laughed, and rocked herself backwards, her arms embracing her knees.

"I feel very like going mad to-night, Kate Hall; now just answer me, is it not terrible to have a bad old man in the house, abusing one abominably to the doctors and servants, and to know that if he gets well, there will be a regular shindy again about my marrying him."

"But, you know, you need never marry him?"

"Ah, it is very well to talk," said Ella. "Of course I shan't marry him, but you see," and she paused. She did not know how much nor how little Miss Hall understood of her father's affairs, but she was in a very communicative mood, and besides she had faith in Kate Hall. "Now just answer me; is it not terrible to have a bad old man in the house, abusing one? You knew," she said, presently, "my father owed him loads of money, didn't you?"

"I did not *know*. I have certainly heard surmises to that effect."

"It's known by this time all over Alton, and Woodly, too, depend upon it; you can't keep secrets with lots of servants about, and a prying gossip like Brimstone Yardly to chatter in every house."

"What! Mr. Yardly, Miss Ella?"

"Oh, how delightfully shocked you look; it's jolly to see your face. Why Brimstone Yardly, he's always talking about brimstones, so I call him by that name; I hate him."

Then Ella was silent for a few minutes; presently she began again:

"I wonder how the poor young Dominie gets on, and whether *he* has heard the gossip about Mr. Thorpe and the money matters? I think I should like to take some more Latin lessons; it would be awfully jolly."

Kate Hall looked up, and her cheek visibly flushed, but Ella's back was turned.

"I think that man is desperately spooney on me."

"I hope not," said Kate Hall, the words came from her involuntarily.

"Why not?" said Ella, facing about.

"Because," said Catherine, cutting her cotton off short, though she had only just threaded her needle, "it would be a sad thing for him to love one who only mocked at his affection."

"How caustic gentle Kate has grown," said Ella, in surprise; "almost as waspish as my original in the charade."

"Why?"

"Super dainty Kate, is that you I hear taking up the cudgels for a young man? Oh, fie! what would Mr. Yardly say?"

Kate laughed a little, and tried to turn the subject.

"No, no," said Ella, "I won't be put off, 'I commence to feel a rat,' as my French governess used to say, that woman was a duffer at English. You take an immense interest in the Dominie, Kate Hall—what if you make a match of it?"

Kate sewed on silently and quickly.

"I would not wonder if it could not be done, but not yet, Kate. I must have a little sport with him first; he is desperately spooney on me, and it's awfully jolly, as I remarked before, to have a party reddening and stammering as he does sometimes."

"I hope you are quite mistaken," said

Miss Hall, rather hotly; "and if not, I must say I consider your conduct unfeeling in the extreme."

Ella actually stood up in astonishment, at hearing the meek companion speak thus.

"Why, Miss Hall—it is not you making those impertinent observations?" but Ella's white teeth gleamed, and her eyes shone kindly. "*You are in love with the schoolmaster of Alton!*"

"Miss Thorpe," said Kate, "if your words were true, it would be ungenerous to speak them; but, remember, I have hardly spoken more than three times to Mr. Cruize in my life."

"Ah! but what may not have transpired during those three times? I begin to fancy the great fellow is a Lothario in his way. I shall warn old Brimstone of his dangerous under-strapper. I shall, he must be a flirt, just like that wretched Darling Challoner," and at the remembrance of Hubert, Ella became grave again. "He was the greatest flirt in Europe, Miss Hall; I wonder he did not make some sweet speeches to you even; I feel confident now, that he made love to Clara Elliot and Bobbie Kilruderey. I really was spooney about that creature—he was a vain, foolish, conceited thing, didn't you think so?"

"I had no opportunity of judging," said Kate, discreetly.

"What a stick you are, Miss Hall, you have no more life than a cabbage plant, except where the Dominie is concerned."

"But really, Miss Thorpe, you see I know nothing, I *can* know nothing about Mr. Challoner."

"Of course not, I suppose you never noticed how he used to lead me off into the shrubbery for hours, and lean over the piano when I played, looking like a cherubim or seraphim, or a Cupid or Adonis, which ever simile suits your taste the best."

Kate Hall was silent; much as she admired Ella's beauty, and that certain amount of frankness in her manner which had won her over at first, she was beginning *to respect her less ;* her clear sighted eyes were opening to certain points in her character which pleased her not; humbly born as she was, there was an intuitive refinement in Kate Hall, which made her prize, above rubies, all feminine qualities and womanly gentleness; and in these it seemed to her that Ella was wholly wanting; there might have been another reason too.

"Did you never notice that Mr. Challoner was very devoted to me, Miss Hall?"

"Not more to you than to the other young ladies, Miss Ella."

Ella was in a rage.

"You are a regular stick," she said, rising and pacing the room. "You haven't a spark of sympathy. Nobody has sympathy in this world!"

Kate felt sorry for her.

"I am sure, dear Miss Thorpe, I feel the greatest, the very greatest pity for you; but

I had not the least idea that you cared at all for Mr. Challoner. You see I know so little of the world, and I set down all his attentions, and your conversations and walks with him, to the mere everyday politeness of people in your sphere."

"Did you? well, let me tell you that you are a duffer!"

Catherine Hall rose to leave the room, because, meek as she was, she did not like insult, and she began to think that her presence irritated Ella.

"Are you going away? I thought you were so gentle that you would put up with everything. I find you are vinegar as well as sugar."

Kate Hall turned round.

"I am not; I do not feel at all angry at whatever you may say, Miss Ella, only my presence seems to annoy you."

"Well, yes, it does. You are such a stick. You can go."

And Kate Hall went.

CHAPTER VI.

MR. YARDLY.

MR. JAMES LESLIE stole up the great staircase the next morning, accompanied by Mr. Thorpe.

"Has he slept well?" asked Mr. Leslie.

"Remarkably so, I believe the first good night's rest he has had."

Mr. Thorpe's manner was more affable than it had been the morning before in the library. Mr. Leslie smiled benignly, they crossed the carpeted passages, then gently tapped at the sick man's door; it opened from inside, and a nurse glided back to the great bedstead. The curtains were undrawn, the patient lay ghastly and grim, and with staring eyeballs. When he saw the visitor he shrieked out:—

"What do you want here, you smooth-faced *lie?* I know you would murder any man for five pounds."

Query—How did the Monster obtain this insight into the character of Mr. Leslie, seeing that he was a complete stranger to him? We can only suppose, that naturally gifted with a peculiar clearness on some points, and with a strange instinct which seldom failed him in detecting the bad qualities of his neighbours, Macnellan's brain must have been sharpened by his fever into more than common keenness, for certainly never was a truer word uttered of any man breathing.

Mr. Leslie walked up to the bed, and smiled pleasantly at the Monster, whereupon the Monster cursed him; then Mr. Leslie laughed softly, and shook his hand close to Macnellan's eyes; they dimmed visibly after that stroke, but he made an effort to speak—

"How dare that villain Thorpe bring you here with your devilish arts? You—"

But again the fat, white hand of Leslie went close to the patient's face, and then he made some rapid passes close to his lips, and the man struggled in vain for utterance. Afterwards Leslie went up to him, and waved his arm over him three or four times. When he left him, Macnellan was in a half dose with a placid, contented expression on his face.

"Now," said Leslie, turning briskly towards Thorpe, "I think we may leave him. Do you allow him much air?" and he walked to the window, which was a French one, and unbolted it and opened the one half of it quite wide. He then stepped out on the balcony which ran round that side of the house, and inhaled the keen frosty air which blew over the snow-covered country;—a strange act of hardihood in one who liked warmth and comfort as he did, but strange as it was, there Mr. Leslie stood, looking towards the fields, the whitened woods, and the blue far hills, where the ruddy light of a fine winter's day painted the sky with gold; then he leant over the balcony, and saw that there was another below him on the next story. What a luxurious home Alton Hall was! Ah! what more right had Thorpe than he to such a place, and what more right had his gipsy stepdaughter, unladylike and queer, to greater happiness than his own soft-mannered, blue-eyed Pauline? Ah! well; he sighed a little, and came into the room with his usual smile.

"I don't think we can bear that window open," said Mr. Thorpe; "the nurse and my wife, I mean, and I am often here, and I dread neuralgia."

"Ah! well," said Leslie, closing it, "but I would open it from time to time; nothing like air."

Then they descended into the library, and Mr. Thorpe stirred the fire, and asked Leslie to sit down, which the latter did.

"I am sure we are very much obliged to

you," said Thorpe. "This kind of illness is hard to deal with."

"Mesmerism is a wonderful discovery," said Leslie.

"Well, I have never thought much about it," said Mr. Thorpe, "but there must be something in it, I suppose."

"You have had proof, I should think, Mr. Thorpe," said Leslie, laughing.

Thorpe was silent. He was wondering if Leslie expected payment for his services, and afraid of offending his delicacy by mentioning it; and so he did not mention it, but showed the Mesmeriser out soon after without any further notice than an exchanged promise to come again.

Leslie walked away,—the smile faded from his lips, his brow gathered into a frown,—he passed through the park, crushed the snow with his heel—perhaps circulation was not quick in him, for soon his fingers ached with cold, and he put them into the pockets of his great-coat to warm them, although he moved at a very brisk pace. Soon the iron gates closed behind him and he was out upon the road, almost ankle-deep in snow, where icicles hung on the hedges, and starving robin red-breasts hopped boldly in his pathway, beseeching a crumb of comfort; but Leslie had few crumbs of comfort of his own then, so he never noticed the robins but just kept on walking fast, wrapping up his hands and shutting his teeth against the north-east wind which blew bitterly over the country side. Presently another tramp was heard approaching him, he looked forward—Mr. Yardly, the Vicar of Alton, was upon him in another moment.

"Good day," said the Vicar, extending his hand, which Leslie took and shook and dropped, "seasonable weather."

Leslie was all smiles again by this time.

"I have just been up to Alton Hall."

"Ah!"

"Making myself useful in regard to that gentleman of whom you told me."

"Indeed!"

"Yes; you would never guess in what way, Mr. Yardly."

Mr. Yardly's plump face of fifty years' standing, with his keen eyes opened to their widest extent, would have served for a "study" of *male* curiosity, which is sometimes as eager in its kind as female.

"You would never guess in what way, and perhaps you would put me under your ban if I told you."

"But may I ask in what way?"

"Most certainly," said Leslie, laughing, "I go there to mesmerise Mr. Macnellan."

The clergyman coughed and looked properly horrified.

"I know you consider that practice wrong."

"Under the circumstances," said the Vicar, "I can hardly express what my feelings are on the subject, Mr. Leslie."

"Oh dear! you won't offend me in the least," said Leslie.

"Then I must say I consider the practice

wrong in the extreme. If there is nothing in it, it is imposture—if there *is*, why so much the worse, it can be but one of the devices of Satan."

"Well," said Leslie, pleasantly, "I can gain nothing by it if it is imposture. I was solely actuated by humane motives, Mr. Yardly, and hearing of the ravings of this poor man, I went to offer what I knew would do him good; I have seen so many patients cured by mesmerism. And as to the old gentleman you alluded to, I hope he has nothing to do with me. Ha! ha!"

Mr. Yardly might have doubted that assertion had he known Leslie as well as we do.

"I hope not, indeed," said Mr. Yardly, shaking his head and putting on his most solemn air. "We all need care, Mr. Leslie, lest we fall into the snares of the enemy."

"But mesmerism is a *science*, my dear sir. Properly understood, in time it will become the most efficacious means of curing diseases."

The Vicar shook his head and looked dreadfully sad.

"It's really cold standing here," said Leslie. "You are not coming my way?"

"I was returning home after a walk," said Mr. Yardly, "but I will turn with you again if you do not object."

Of course Leslie did not object, and he and the Vicar faced about towards Woodly.

"And how does Mr. Macnellan seem?" asked the Vicar.

"Better, infinitely better."

"Does he rave as he did?" asked Mr. Yardly, in a very soft voice, but with ears open for any news.

"A little; but the mesmerism has a wonderful effect."

"Does he allude to the money transactions?"

"Not so much, I think."

"There is some truth then in the report, I suppose?"

"No doubt of it," said Leslie, confidentially (though he knew nothing about it).

"I wonder to what extent poor Thorpe is involved," mused the Vicar, sighing.

"To an immense amount I am positive," said Leslie; and again the Vicar opened his eyes.

"And is Miss Thorpe really unwilling for the match?"

"She swears she won't have him," said Leslie, who as yet had not spoken to Ella.

"Hardened girl," said the Vicar, vehemently—he had a particular antipathy to Ella—"What does she expect? Have you heard anything extraordinary about her going away?"

Leslie had only heard it from Yardly himself, besides he was afraid of saying too much, knowing his customer too well.

"I think that is all a report," said he.

Then the Vicar lowered his head, he spoke at last: "Extracrdinary that people will spend such sums in jewellery. Why that Mrs. Thorpe has thirty thousand pounds worth of diamonds, as I told you last week. One begins to doubt if Thorpe has paid for them all."

"Perhaps not," said Leslie.

"He is very extravagant, that is an incontestible fact," said the Vicar, and he was silent again.

Just then Crane's farm came in sight, and the Vicar turned, and rejecting Mr. Leslie's invite to enter his house, he shook him by the hand, and went back to Alton. Mr. Yardly was as proud in his way as Mr. Thorpe. His wife and daughters never descended to intimacy with unknown people like the Leslies. They were rich, and lived in comfort and luxury, and they gave very little to the poor except advice and tracts; they thought, and so did Mr. Yardly, that very very few would enter heaven, but they felt a comforting assurance that they were among the select number. Mr. Yardly did not do very much visiting on the whole, among the poor—he had left it off since the arrival of his Curate, who was indefatigable in that line. He visited the rich a great deal; he had an inveterate love of gossip, so had his wife and daughters; they were not liked, they were too severe in their judgments, too stingy with their purses, too unbending to their inferiors, to be liked. Mr. Yardly took a great interest in Sunday Schools; he liked to have plenty of under-strappers teaching in them. He had not been more than two years Vicar of Alton before the arrival of Martin, but had established two schools. When he sent Martin down to Thorpe's to beg old histories, it was not so much to instil general historical facts in the children's minds, as to impress upon them the date of the Reformation and the persecutions under Mary. He did not get along at all well with his Curate, their ideas clashed on all points; he was all for justice, Clyne was all for mercy. He gave tracts but no soup, and it was like a reproach to him that Clyne gave far more away out of his scanty stipend than he did out of his rich living and private fortune. Then he considered that Clyne had terribly lax notions on some points; he almost feared that his Curate believed in a universal redemption, than which nothing would have grieved the Vicar more, had it been true even; for he was so fond of justice, that he could not bear to think that all the careless people round him were not to be burnt for their forgetfulness one day; he saw so many going straight away to perdition, *he* knew so well *where* they were going that it was useless to talk to *him*. He entered Alton at about twelve, he passed his own beautiful house, which lay to the left across some fields, and went down to the school-house to have some talk with the master, with whose conduct lately he had been much dissatisfied. He found the children flocking noisily out; they stopped and pulled their forelocks, and then skulked on timidly. Martin was just locking the room when his superior came up; he bowed to him, and waited to hear what he had to say.

"Mr. Cruize, I wish to speak with you."

Martin faced about with a dull expression.

"I will walk with you down to your lodgings, Mr. Cruize; I am sorry to hear from Mrs. King that you still owe her thirty shillings from your last quarter."

"I can't help it, Mr. Yardly."

"That is just what all people say, who get into debt. You can't help it, it is extraordinary that you cannot live on forty pounds a year. Do you assist your mother?"

"It is very difficult to live on forty pounds a year, I assure you, sir," said the schoolmaster, evading the question of the Vicar.

"Yes, if people won't learn to be economical, of course it is; I am afraid you are very extravagant."

"Sir?"

Martin chafed under this irritating interference, and inwardly cursed his captivity, and perhaps his Vicar also.

"Has Mr. Leslie paid you yet?"

"No, sir."

"Why, how much does he owe you?"

"About ten pounds. I have left off going

there since November. Mrs. Leslie told me I had better not come any more."

"Ten pounds," said the Vicar, "from May to November, why that's five pounds a quarter."

"Yes, sir."

"An immense sum," said the Vicar, "why dear me, you might have known they never meant to pay that."

The Viçar got all his teaching done very cheaply. There was a hard working young lady who walked over from a neighbouring village and instructed his two younger children in grammar, geography, writing and arithmetic, for an hour a day, and he paid her thirty shillings a quarter.*

Thus he was amazed at the price Martin had charged the Leslies.

"Why, you know, you really would be ashamed to put Leslie in the court; the Judge would laugh at such a preposterous charge."

Martin's hands tingled, cold as was the

* This is no fiction.

weather, and a sensation like cold water trickling among the roots of his hair warned him that he was in a rage.

"Leslie offered the terms himself," he said sulkily.

"No doubt," said the Vicar, with an unpleasant smile, "but we know Mr. Leslie never troubles himself to pay anybody. He is dreadfully in debt at St. Jude's. I know of five shops between which he owes a hundred and fifty pounds. By the way, what was your impression about that Miss Pauline French? Do you think she is really Mrs. Leslie's daughter?"

"I don't know."

"Do they quarrel much?"

"I don't know."

"Does not Leslie devote himself to her in a very extraordinary way?"

"I don't know, sir," said Martin, obstinately.

The Vicar was balked—then he said suddenly:—

"Have the Thorpes paid you?"

"I have not sent my bill in."

"What did you charge them?"

"I think it was three pounds a month."

"You think; but really, Mr. Cruize, you are old enough to look after your own affairs better than that—such an enormous charge, too—you could not presume more if you had had a university education."

Again the cold water trickled about Martin's head.

They now entered his sitting-room, where the fire was just lighted, and the room full of smoke, and Martin opened the window. Mr. Yardly coughed, then he said:—

"You must send Mr. Thorpe's bill in at once; but you really must not charge all that. Five pounds will be all you need charge; make it out now, while I sit here, and I'll go up to-morrow and tell Mrs. Thorpe you are in need of money to pay your rent, and she will pay it."

Take money for the dearest delight his life

had known—the teaching of Ella—and be humiliated in her eyes. Never, never! though ten thousand Yardlys walked into his room, and gave him insulting orders.

"Make it out now, Mr Cruize."

"No thank you, sir, I would rather ask for my money myself."

"But I tell you I would rather get it for you, and tell Mrs. Thorpe of your distress."

"I don't choose," said Martin, drawing himself up, and looking fiercely at his patron, "I don't choose Mrs. Thorpe to know that I am in debt. I don't intend her to know it at all."

The Vicar reddened; this insubordination on the part of a dependent was dreadful.

"You forget who you are speaking to," said Mr. Yardly.

"No, I don't," said Martin, recklessly, "I know quite well that you are the Vicar of Alton, and I am the schoolmaster, and that you could turn me out in March, or even perhaps next week, at Christmas; but still I will not have your interference in my private affairs. You have nothing to do with my debts or my bills."

"You speak very intemperately because you are in a rage," said Mr. Yardly. "I always look upon passion as a species of madness; but I see perfectly that you are not a fit person for the office you have undertaken. You leave me, Mr. Cruize, at the March quarter. You shall have a written notice to-morrow, and understand," added the Vicar, "that I will have your bills paid. I shall not pay you another farthing, until I have seen you clear; in fact, I shall pay Mrs. King, and the rest of your bills, before I pay you."

"Then I can force you to pay me all over again," said Martin, "and I will. I shall then put you in the court, Mr. Yardly."

Martin trembled with passion. The Vicar vouchsafed him no reply, but walked out of the room, not out of the house, however. He went into the kitchen, where Mrs. King enlivened him with gossip, and liberal abuse of Martin, and Martin had to go to afternoon school with only half a dinner, so long did the saintly Vicar detain his landlady.

CHAPTER VII.

LATIN AGAIN.

"MAMMA, isn't Arthur coming home?" asked Ella, three days before Christmas, when she sat in the drawing-room one evening after dinner.

"No, I thought it would be so dull for the poor fellow; he couldn't enjoy himself with this patient in the house."

"We could give him a good mount, and he glories in hunting."

"But he likes home sports too; he's going to stay at Railcroft, with Hubert Challoner's brother; they will have a merry house full there."

"I wish I could go," said Ella, sighing, "but still it wouldn't do for me to meet that precious darling; we had a quarrel, you know, a regular out and outer."

"Absurd," said Mrs. Thorpe, "but it won't do for you to leave just yet, because Macnellan asks for you so often."

"Do you think there's any chance of his getting the right side of Jordan soon?"

"I'm sure I can't say. This mesmerism quiets him wonderfully; I almost think he will recover."

"What a fluke."

"What?"

"A fluke. We don't want him to recover, and yet we take such pains to nurse him up; we must, too. It would be awful if we didn't take care of him, because if he died we should never be easy again, if it was in the least our faults."

"No," assented Mrs. Thorpe, who was knitting a pretty scarf to tie round the lap-dog's neck.

Ella was in her favourite posture on a low seat, with her arms embracing her knees. She felt bored to death with the life she was leading, and her mind would recur in spite of herself to her wild adventure in Yanston, Cumberland.

"I saw such an extraordinary thing in the *Illustrated News* to day," said Mrs. Thorpe. "Bring it here, Ella, and read it yourself, one of the oddest things I ever read."

Ella brought the paper, her mother found the place, and she read as follows:—

"EXTRAORDINARY WEDDING.

"About three weeks since a lady drove up to a small public house in the village of Yanston, Cumberland, about a mile from the Railway Station, and having walked into the bar where a few villagers were smoking, she said to the assembled rustics, 'I will give one hundred pounds to anybody who will marry me to-morrow morning.'

"Incredulity and strong suspicions of the

lady's sanity were the first thoughts of her hearers, but the lady with distinct utterance assured them of her sanity, and repeated her offer, but she made the extraordinary stipulation that the person who married her should sign a paper promising never to seek her again. She kept her face covered the whole of the time. It would seem that there was only one unmarried man in the company, the nephew of a small farmer in the neighbourhood, and he signed the paper, and the lady then retired to her room for the night. The landlord went that night to the clergyman, who happened to have a license in his house, and the next morning the pair were wed. The villager took his money and was immediately rid of his queer bride, whose face he had not seen, and who returned by the next train to London. The lady's name does not transpire, but if any of our readers should have the curiosity to search the register, and inquire the name of the Yanston rustic, perhaps they may discover that this weird bride was a princess, or duchess, or an earl's daughter in disguise."

Ella's face paled and flushed by turns as she read this, but her mother was too busy with her own thoughts to watch her countenance. When she could command her voice she said:

"They always put those things to fill up the papers; it is like the ripe gooseberries and cooked steaks falling from the clouds in a shower of rain. You know we read of that."

"Live fish you mean, Ella," said Mrs. Thorpe. "I never heard of cooked steaks."

"I think I read of something quite as wonderful. If it wasn't steaks it was meat pies or bottles of champagne."

Thus Ella turned from the subject, but horrible surmises were rife in her mind. What if some of her kind friends, the Darling or the Kilrudereys were to suspect her of this wild act, and send to Yanston to know the name out of curiosity? But, no; people never did those things. They might read it and laugh, and say, "I wonder if that's Ella Thorpe, it's just like her?" and then they would forget all about it. Nobody would ever go to Cumberland to see for themselves, and now she was safe from the monster if ever he recovered again, and free—free as the winds! She was married, so she might go anywhere if it were necessary. And yet, poor thing, while she told herself she was free as the winds, here she was tied down to a dull home still at the monster's pleasure, without one single thing to amuse her except a scamper across the country on the back of black Fan, and from that she was prevented by the frost.

"It's awfully dull, mamma," she said at length. "Let me have the schoolmaster again to teach me Latin?"

"You may if you like."

"May he come to-morrow?"

"Yes, if you like."

The next morning a message was sent up to Martin, with whom it was holiday time now, that Miss Thorpe would be glad to continue her Latin lessons, if he would come to the Hall at about eleven. And Martin received the message at his breakfast hour, and was strongly agitated in consequence. He had not seen her since—since when? since she had become his lawful wife in the sight of men, and of God! His wife!—was this mocking spirit his wife? Could it be possible that now his long cherished oath might be fulfilled, and none dare to say him nay? How should he comport himself when in her presence? And he pictured scenes in which, falling on his knees he should claim her as his own, and swear by all the powers of light and darkness she should never leave him. And she, what would she do? turn white and shriek, and run to her parents for protection from her common lowly husband?

Then Martin went and dressed himself in his best clothes, and arranged his dark hair to the best advantage, and he stood before the little cracked glass in his bed-chamber, and contemplated his own countenance. It was plain, decidedly it was plain, was the judgment he formed on it—the eyebrows were shaggy and joined too closely; the nose was too short, the jaw too massive; the eyes were remarkable and keen, and now, lighted by the fires of passion, they were almost fine; but the complexion was destitute of colouring, it was of an opaque whiteness, without being fair. As yet, he had scarcely any hair on his face, and the poor fellow was weak enough to whisper to himself that, perhaps, when his whiskers should be grown, he would be a handsomer man; he was enormously tall. Did Ella admire height? No, that fair haired doll she had seemed so fond of, was short, and how was it he had not married her? Martin, by some strange chance, was ignorant that it was the invalid whom Ella had been about to marry! He had not been to the Leslies nor to the Higlys lately, and had heard no gossip.

At eleven o'clock he rang the bell at Alton Hall, and was shown into the memorable breakfast-parlour. The gorgeous flowers on the tapestry carpet seemed to speak yet of the days of the past summer, when flowers as bright had bloomed upon the lawn. Now all without was comfortless; but a fire burnt in the low grate, a few fine paintings enlivened the walls, the splendid French clock still ticked upon the mantel-shelf, some hot-house flowers were in a white and gold vase of Bohemian glass on the sideboard, the room seemed the abode of comfort, luxury, beauty.

The schoolmaster stood near the table waiting; then the door opened softly, not as Ella would have swung it open, and Miss Hall, in one of her dark morning dresses, glided into the room. Martin bowed and felt vexed—she had extended her hand, then seeing Martin's cold salute and almost angry eye, she grew scarlet and bowed too.

"Miss Thorpe is not yet down," she said,

speaking as though she was hurt, and in a subdued tone; "if you do not object to wait for a short time, she will soon be here?"

Object? Martin wanted to grasp her pale hand now, and thank her for her welcome news. His face lighted up, and he said, kindly:—

"You don't look well, I fancy, Miss Hall!"

"Oh!" said Catherine, smiling in her turn, "people always judge from my pale face. I never had a colour."

It was not *that*; Martin noticed a dark ring under the eye, and the cheek seemed more worn and thinner than usual.

"Perhaps you have been up at night with this invalid," said Martin.

"Only two nights, and not together."

"But you certainly don't look well," said the schoolmaster.

"I think I might return the compliment," said Kate Hall, smiling and drawing her knitting from her pocket; "you don't look well, Mr. Cruize!"

"You and I," said Martin, "don't see the sunny side of life, Miss Hall—we have to walk in the shade and carry our burdens, and we often feel thirsty and there is no water near us. We leave the other side of the hill to bright creatures, like Miss Thorpe and her visitors—they have no burdens to carry, no thirst they cannot quench, for all the brightest fountains of life spring up at their side of the hill, all the flowers bloom there, all the fruits ripen there, and the sun always shines there. It seems a little hard upon us at the dark, barren, steep side, does it not?"

"But we are not sure that we shall have to stay on the barren side always," said Kate, "we, *you*, at least (I don't speak of myself, a woman's sphere is so circumscribed), but you may yet carve out a pathway for yourself, to the other and sunnier side of the hill."

She could talk now that she had a listener who took an interest in what she was saying, and who sympathized with her feelings—Kate was no stick. How is it that men so often say things to women, hoping to please them at the time, and never counting on the consequences? Pity for Catherine and an admiration for her quiet, unobtrusive beauty were the only motives that actuated Martin, when he said:—

"And if I ever did carve out such a path, and you were still on the barren side, I would take you with me."

He only meant if I were rich I would give you a pension, or endow you with a little fortune and marry you to a worthy husband; but Kate only dwelt on the words, and she thought Martin a mirror of truth, so a glow came on her thin cheek, and a light into her sunken eye.

"But, Mr. Cruize," said she gently, and after a pause, "we ought not only to think of the pleasantness or unpleasantness of the road, but of where we are going to."

"Ah, it is all very well for women, children, and priests to think of those things. I confess they are quite beyond my comprehension."

"Mr. Cruize!"

"Do I shock you? But you know the Alton schoolmaster is not obliged to be orthodox. I never teach in the school on Sundays. The children get plenty of heavenly talk from Mr. Yardly then, and his most righteous daughters. You ought to talk to them, Miss Hall, about the final end of the Hill. I have enough to do to think how I can best carry my burden here."

"Because you don't believe in the reality of the end."

"Perhaps not."

Kate sighed.

"You will pray for me?" asked Martin, smiling.

Kate had prayed for him already; was praying for him now, had he but known it.

"I dare say all these things seem very real to you," Martin went on, "to me they are poems, fancies, beautiful when I can read them for myself from the glorious old book of antiquity, but detestable when I hear them from the lips of hard and tyrannical and narrow-minded men, who, because they are priests, take upon themselves to dictate and tell you what God means when they only propound their own prejudices."

"But you believe in God," said Kate nervously.

"Ah, yes, who could doubt that, and look round at this world so beautifully ordered? who could watch the rolling of the year from the fresh greenness of the spring through the gorgeous glories of summer and the golden riches of the autumn to now, when nature lies sleeping under the frosts of winter, and doubt that some 'Mind' must order all this?"

"And the stars and the planets," said Kate Hall.

"Yes, the immensity of the universe proves a great power."

"Then," said Kate, "why doubt the revealed word of that power?"

"It is not the revealed word, it is the imagination of Jewish poets and dreamers."

"And He who died for us?" said Kate, in a low tone of reverence.

"His is the sublimest life, the noblest death I ever read of," said Martin, "and the code of laws He has left us have done more to dignify human nature than any man's laws before or since."

"They were not man's laws," said Kate.

Martin shook his head sadly in token of disbelief, and was silent.

"Why do you doubt?'" said Kate.

"I doubt because the beautiful order which reigns in inanimate nature seems not to extend to the affairs of men; the hard and selfish prosper, the good are crushed beneath the heel of the cruel and the proud. The loving-hearted have none to love them, and the heartless have torrents of love poured out at their feet, the pure and self-sacrificing go through life suffering and lonely, the unscrupulous and wicked go on prospering and to prosper. Death hews down the loved mother, the worshipped wife, the cherished child, and spares, for long years, the unpitying miser who hoards his gold, while breadless infants die daily from want—that is not half nor a quarter of the ills and wrongs to which flesh is heir—this is why I disbelieve."

"But one day," said Kate, "there shall be a righting of wrongs, when the crooked shall be made straight, and the rough places plain; even now if we would have patience and look closely at our own lives and those of others we should find a ruling Providence ordering all things, but we must wait and watch and pray, Mr. Cruize."

At this juncture Ella bounded into the room.

"I've been listening," she said, "for the last ten minutes, and I found the door ajar—what torrents of eloquence you two have been pouring forth," but she did not laugh or even seem amused enough to quiz Martin or Kate. "I had no idea, Mr. Cruize, that you could talk like that; I did not think you had it in you."

Martin's heart gave one great throb when

she entered, and then seemed to stand still. He looked at her more fondly than he had ever dared to look before, and there was a quiet power in the glance that somehow abashed Ella, for she lowered her daring dark eyes for an instant. This Dominie is an odd fish was her thought; then she dragged a chair to the table, before Martin had time to place one for her, and she seated her wilful self observing, "You're not cut out for a drawing-room gallant, Mr. Cruize?"

"Never was any one less so," said Martin.

"You ought to have been standing with this chair in your hand waiting to know where I would have it placed."

"I ought so."

"Instead of which you discuss knotty points with Miss Hall, which in my opinion are far above your comprehension," she flashed her eye upon him as she spoke thus, and a roguish light danced there.

"You have a poor opinion of my comprehension, Miss Thorpe."

"Well perhaps I have, and perhaps I've not," she returned, beginning to turn over the leaves of her grammar. "I've not by any means made up my mind about you yet. I don't know whether I like you, or—" she paused.

"Or—" repeated the schoolmaster.

"Hate you," said Ella, brusquely. And the word uttered half in play struck like a dagger at the heart of Martin Cruize. At one time he would rather have had her hatred, anything than her contempt, but now that he held this dark power over her, and if she came to know it suddenly unpleasantly, how she might learn to loath him!! His face altered so at the idea that Kate Hall, who had looked up more than once in the exercise of the functions of her office as Chaperone, noticed the gloom of his countenance. Just then, however, she was not in a mood to attribute his depression to its right cause.

"Come, Miss Hall," said Ella, "what are you prying about? You talk to the Dominie yourself," she stopped short, the word was out, what could she do but blush red to the roots of her hair, and laugh convulsively?

"That is the name you give me, I suppose," said Martin, smiling.

"Just so, as that mesmerising man Leslie would say. Yes, I usually denominate you 'the Dominie.' I might call you worse names, I'm sure."

"Perhaps you do?"

"No I don't, do I, Miss Hall?"

"Am I to tell the truth?" asked Kate, who was strangely irritated for her, and who looked scarcely like calm sweet Kate at that moment.

"Of course you are," said Ella, roughly; "when do I ask you to tell lies," she would have said, but she thought better of it, and substituted the mild word "fibs."

"Well then I have heard you call Mr. Cruize—"

"Hold your tongue," shouted Ella, waving her hand towards her. "I'll tell him myself. I've called you a muff, because you never seemed up to snuff, nor inclined for a spree. I've called you a stick, because you always seemed as though nothing could move you, and you were only made to say 'yes' and 'no,' and just teach, and take up your hat and go. I've called you a spooney because you've looked, and stammered, and blushed lately as though you were—in short—it must out, spooney on me."

"And now I should think," said Kate Hall, almost violently, "now I should think Miss Ella, that Mr. Cruize would never be what you call spooney on you again?"

"Should you think so indeed?" retorted Ella, "nobody cares what you think, that's one thing."

Poor Kate! how true the words were. Who *did* care what she thought? nor if she fretted her soul out, who on earth cared for her?

And Martin, wrapped up in Ella and in Ella alone, gave his attention solely to her, and hardly heard what Kate had said—"Then," said he, slowly, "I am the Dominie, a muff, a stick, and a spooney," and he smiled, and did not look the least vexed at Ella.

"You were," said Ella, "but since that dressing you gave me in the lumber-room, I've concluded you were neither muff nor stick."

"And spooney?"

"Well, that's as time will show," she answered, coquettishly nodding her naughty head. "And now before the lesson begins, I do wish Miss Hall would step out of the room for five minutes, I want to speak privately to you."

Thereupon Kate Hall, not without secret misgivings that she was doing wrong, gathered up her work and hurried from the room, closing the door tightly after her. Martin waited with breathless interest to hear what she would say. Then she began in a soft, almost shy little whisper:

"Mr. Cruize, Brimstone Yardly was here yesterday, talking about you; he said you were impertinent and wild, and that you owed debts, and that you had charged us much more than you had any right to charge for my lessons, and that he hoped mamma would cut you down in the price when you sent your bill in, and only give you five pounds instead of the nine or ten we owe you."

Martin gulped down his rage against Brimstone Yardly as best he could, but he found Ella's eyes resting kindly on him, and it comforted him greatly.

"And so," continued Ella, "since I know mamma always does try to save what she can, because papa spends all he can, I've been afraid that you might come off badly when the accounts were settled, and so look here" —she dived into her pocket, and pulled out a glittering purse, "I had my quarter's allowance yesterday, much more than I shall spend this winter, shut up with this sick monster in the house, so do take these five sovereigns," and she put them into his hand, "I can't bear you to be cheated, and I'm so jolly glad you gave it well to old Brimstone; you've gone up eighty degrees in my esteem since I heard that."

Inwardly blessing the gentleman irreverently styled Brimstone for that quarrel which had made Ella think better of him, and almost suffocated with love and gratitude, Martin remained without speaking for full a minute, but his eyes spoke for him, and Ella quite shrunk away from their brightness and fire.

"What a queer fellow he is," she thought within herself.

"Miss Thorpe," he said, "call me spooney or not, but I never intended to have sent in a bill at all. Giving you instruction has been so pleasant to me—"

"And I have chaffed, bullied, and teased you out of your life."

"As it is your nature to do to all with whom you come in contact—but you have not annoyed me in the least."

"Not in the lumber-room?"

"No."

"You seemed angry."

"I was not."

"You bullied *me* then."

"Yes, in a dastardly manner." Here he put the five sovereigns down upon the table. "I can't take this money."

"You muff."

"I can't indeed."

"Then Brimstone was a liar when he said you were poor, it's not true?"

"It is quite true."

"That you owe that wretched old Mrs. King for rent—"

"Not only that, but, at a shop in St. Jude's for my boots, and a little at my butcher's. I am as poor as a rat."

"Then do take this money."

"No, no, I could not rob you of your allowance; but, God bless you!"

"Hypocrite!"

"Why?" in an alarmed voice.

"Did I not hear you tell Miss Hall that

though God ruled the universe, he had no care for men? and yet you bid him bless me."

"It is a habit to invoke the care of the All Powerful on the heads of those we love," faltered Martin. And then that impish Ella spoilt the effect of her kindness by bursting into a wild elfish laugh, and shouting "Muff, spooney, put that money into your pocket, for mercy's sake, and don't look sentimental. What a drawing your head would make for a scene from the sorrows of Werter, or, better still—Augustus Moddle, love-sick for Mercy Pecksniff. Put that money into your pocket, or I'll call Miss Hall, and she'll open her saucer eyes, and it will get round to old Brimstone, and there'll be *the deuce* to pay."

It was the first time Martin had heard her rap out an oath. He did not like the sound, but he put the money in his pocket, and then she went into the passage and shouted to Miss Hall, and Kate came down with a passive face, and then the lesson commenced in earnest.

That evening, as Ella was retiring for the

night, her maid put a small parcel into her hand. It was heavy. She went to her room and broke the seal, when out rolled her five sovereigns, but no word or line of any kind.

"Heaven help that Dominie!" said Ella, "he is a perfect cure."

CHAPTER VIII.

VICAR AND CURATE.

A FEW days after Christmas the frost broke up, the snow melted, the rain fell in torrents, and the wind rose in its rudest manner, and went about like a great rough giant out of temper, doing all the bullying blustering things it could, tearing up trees, breaking down branches, rattling the slates off the poor folks' cottages, howling down chimneys, shrieking at house corners, blowing in the faces of pedestrians, lifting little children off their legs, turning women's cloaks over their heads, carrying men's hats out of their reach, and now and then toppling down a house stack with infinite danger to life and limb. The wind always irritated Mrs. King, Martin's landlady, and she was in a very ill humour because the kitchen chimney smoked, although, as her quiet husband told her, it was the best thing in the world for drying the ground for seeds, not to speak of the week's washing, which was already fit for the mangle. But Mrs. King only thought of the smoke, and ignored the clothes and the seeds.

Martin had paid her, for Mrs. Thorpe had asked for his bill, and he had written to tell her to pay him what she liked, and so she had sent him seven pounds, and he was tolerably comfortable now. He was indulging himself with a number of "All the Year Round," borrowed from the St. Jude's library, and waiting for his dinner.

Martin began to feel hungry at last. An hour after his time he rang his bell, and Mrs. King came in blustering with wrath, like the wind itself. She was a thin woman, with a white face, something of a shrew, much of a gossip. She considered herself rather a superior person, because her father had been a Wesleyan minister (but he had died in her infancy), and her daughter was married to a small draper at St. Jude's. I forgot to state that her husband was a nursery man, and was by no means badly off. She had a sharp, high, rasping voice when she was angry, and once offended, Mrs. King was an implacable enemy, though she was rather a kind friend when she was a friend, and Martin would have been wise had he conciliated her more.

"I suppose you want your dinner, Mr. Cruize?" said Mrs. King, in a bitter sarcastic tone.

"If you please, Mrs. King."

"My pleasing ain't got much to do with it, Mr. Cruize, the chimly smokes so that I can't cook nothin'; you must find fault with the wind not with me. The sut blows that thick down the fire place there's no boiling, roasting, nor frying."

"Then can't you let me have the toasting fork and a dish here, and I'll toast myself some ham, and that will do quite well."

"To tell you the truth, Mr. Cruize, I never was used to having my carpets greased with cooking. I've been used to a deal, but I've not been used to that."

"Then," said Martin (who certainly since he had been in love had become a bad tempered fellow), "you mean to say you won't let me have any dinner? I shall go and get mine at the inn."

"And tell the company there as your landlady won't cook for you, I warrant you," and here Mrs. King's voice grew sharper and sharper.

"Yes," said Martin, bluntly. "I shall tell the people, of course, that you won't cook for me, or can't, or something," and he rustled his blue covered periodical and pretended to read away fiercely.

"And lay the blame of everything to my housekeeping. See if I don't let Mr. Yardly know how fond you are of that there public house!"

Martin began to whistle, stirred the fire, and made a great fuss with the fire-irons, but high above the noise he made, rose the shrill treble of the virtuously indignant Mrs. King.

"See if I don't let him know you spend two nights a week in that there bar!"

Still Martin whistled a popular air and gave furious pokes to the fire, and still Mrs. King's voice rose above the din in sharpest treble key.

"And takes your glass of spirits hot a'most every night,"—(this was untrue).

Down fell poker, shovel, and tongs with a crash that would have made a less bold woman start.

"And has behaved to me, a respectable married 'ooman, as no man as calls hisself a man would do," whereupon Martin yawned, and prepared to put on his cap and overcoat.

"A swearin drinkin fellah." Martin tugged on his coat, "as makes no more account of a woman's feelings nor if she was a block of granate stone." Martin buttoned his coat. "And as sends love letters to young ladies as his above him, a making a fool of hisself if ever there was one." And Mrs. King laughed a laugh of hideous scorn.

Martin left off whistling, and listened to her.

"A giving letters to Miss Thorpe's maid, knowing Miss Thorpe to be a lady, and hisself no more account than the dirt beneath her feet."

Martin's self-command forsook him just when he stood most in need of it. He faced about on Mrs. King.

"You chattering idiot," said he furiously, "be careful what you say."

"A chattering hidiot I may be," returned Mrs. King, "which low abuse of me, a respectable married 'ooman, as never took insults from nobody, shall be repeated word for word to the Vicar if ever I live to see another day, and also Mr. Yardly shall know of your writin to Miss Thorpe, which Fanny can prove upon her hoath, if needful."

Mrs. King had a son, a miller, near Woodly; he was Fanny's lover, and thus Martin stood condemned. The packet with the five sovereigns had been entrusted to Fanny, whom Martin had met in the village the afternoon of the day that he had received the money.

"Say what you like about me," said Martin, "but don't mention Miss Thorpe's name for the world;" which was the silliest thing he could have said, for thereupon Mrs. King determined that the village should ring with the name of Miss Thorpe.

"A young lady as is'nt above making a fool of a plough-boy or a carter, if she could get her fun out of him, and *she* may do what she likes. But for a *dirty bit* of a *village schoolmaster*" (these words given with a tone in attempting to describe which the expressions withering, bitter, scornful, are weak and inadequate) "a dirty bit of a schoolmaster to make hisself a general laughing stock, is most absurd."

Martin went out of the house and banged the door as loudly as he could, which was childish of him. In the village he met Richard Higly, the youngest brother of the farmer where Kate had been governess. Richard was the worst type of the genus English farmer of which there are so many good excellent types, I am confident; but Richard was all that Mrs. King represented Martin, and worse, much worse,—drunken—so that his intemperance broke out in his face in red blotches and swelled nose;—a swearer, and more, a blasphemer; for, as we have seen, Kate Hall had left his sister-in-law's house in consequence of his and his brother's language. Ignorant, vulgar, brutal, uncharitable, coarse, unpitying, without one good aspiration, without the least respect for goodness, with no understanding of it, with no reverence for anything but *money*. Those who were rich he certainly was very civil to, and he had a sort of crouching way towards the gentry, which might have sprung from something like fear. As I write, the original of Richard rises dimly before my eyes; the mists clear, and I see him as I saw him in my childhood, and judged him with a child's unerring instinct, without prejudice either, for he never was unkind to me. How brutal he was to animals! how he would beat a sparrow's brains out against his wooden chair, if the cat brought one in as yet unhurt, repeating some doggrel rhyme about shooting or striking, and when he came to the telling word, thump, thump, would go the little head against the chair-rail—faugh! and then he would tie a kettle to a dog's tail, and lash it out of the yard; and how badly-off came the younger farm boys, such as could not defend themselves—how he would swear at them and strike them! This Richard had a silly dressy wife (the Higly's were quite rich people) whom sometimes he used to amuse himself by knocking down stairs. She had been a young woman of spirit, but her husband tamed her completely. The two sisters-in-law lived together, quarrelled copiously, and made it up again. The brothers seldom disagreed—they did not care a half-penny for each other, but they got on well with the joint stock farming, one relieved the other—they made heaps of money; their cheeses were the best in the parish; they were the veriest Mammon worshippers the sun ever shone upon. I think the farmers Fielding painted must have been exact types of these Higlys; they were a century and a half behind their time. They were hospitable; they thought much of good living—and here, I suppose, was their redeeming point. Yes, let me do them justice, they were *very* hospitable. I think a dinner party, and a good drunken bout afterwards, with the neighbouring farmers, was their keenest appreciation of enjoyment. The wives could then don satins and gold chains, and vie with the wives of other farmers in the richness of their clothes. The men could talk of pigs, potatoes, turnips and cheese, and intersperse their conversation with ribaldry and noise—and then they could drink! Poor fellows, they are dead now; they died young. No constitutions could stand a long course of such intemperance.

"Art going to the Falcon," demanded Richard?

"Yes," said Martin, "I am going to get my dinner there. My landlady won't cook for me to-day; her chimney smokes.

"If you're a going out for your dinner, you may as well come up to the Oak Farm, we've some fine cider." And so Martin turned with Richard across the fields towards the Oak Farm.

"You're a going away, I heard," said Richard, with a wink, "what's thee been up to?"

"I told Mr. Yardly not to interfere with my affairs, that's all."

"The parson's a—" we won't write down what Richard said. Nobody likes now-a-days to read filthy words.

Martin did not look disgusted at Dick Higly's words; he was not going to let him know that he was at all anxious or unhappy, or poor. He knew the Higly's had not much sympathy with unhappy people, it was necessary to appear tolerably jolly in their company, they would not have lent ten or twenty or even five pounds, to save a fellow creature's life, but they would give a good dinner to any one who could afford to pay for one elsewhere, and who could tell them some news, and smoke a pipe with them, and it entered into the thick head of Richard Higly that it would be good fun to make the steady-going young schoolmaster helplessly drunk—this was one of the pastimes in which he most delighted.

"We've splendid cider," said Dick.

"Last year's?" said Martin, trying to take an interest in what the other was saying.

"Four year old," said Richard.

Here they came upon the great farm yard, with its immense barns and, stacks, and cow-sheds, a little green plot, enclosed with white rails, was in front of the house, and protected it from the dirt of the yard.

The house was of the style called "Elizabethan," with pointed gabled front, mullioned windows, with tiny diamond panes, and a heavy black oak door, covered with nobs. It had been a house of some importance two hundred years before; it was coloured with yellow cement, and had a really imposing appearance in its way; the back of it looked into a large well-kept garden, where the paths were made of turf instead of gravel, where rich dahlias bloomed on a little green lawn in the autumn, where there were pear trees and scarlet runners in the summer, where there was an arbour, and where there were hives for bees. Against one side of the house, too, there grew peaches and apricots; this garden was surrounded with low hedges of hawthorn, which separated it from the adjoining fields, and now Martin and Richard pushed back the oak door with the black nobs, and entered a stone passage scrupulously clean; there was a door opposite, leading into the garden, but this door was closed on the windy day in question; on the left hand was a large kitchen, where the farm servants eat, and where the good dinners were cooked; the door of this place stood ajar, and Martin caught a glimpse of a great fire roaring up the wide chimney, and a large turkey turning round before it on a roasting jack, but Richard ushered him into another room on the right hand; this was flagged with large, smooth, whitened stones, it was a spacious room with a long, low, mullioned window looking into the garden, and a smaller and more modern one looking into the front court. This room was pannelled with dark polished wood, the chairs were of the same; there was a clawed oak table in the centre covered with a spotless damask cloth, and glasses, and knives and forks were laid neatly upon it, and a silver flagon for cider, presented to the Higlys' father (dead since), by the members of the Alton Hunt Club, of which he had been a distinguished member. The Higlys were great at all field sports. There was an enormous fire in the wide chimney place, and the whole house seemed to speak of good and warmth, and well-doing in a worldly sense of the word. Richard went to the foot of the wide oak stair case, the ballustrades of which even were richly carved, and shouted "Missus come down."

"What is that man bawling for?" said a voice behind Martin; he turned in time to go and shake Mrs. John Higly by the hand, and ask her how she was. Mrs. John had just come in from the dairy; she was a woman of thirty-five, dark as a gipsey, with large, ill-formed nose, wide mouth, small, sulky black eyes, and a forehead, a nail's breadth in length, literally no more, and the thick, coarse, coal-black hair was braided over it, and all but touched the eyes. She was a larged-boned woman of middle height, almost ugly, because the expression of her face was so malevolent; once offend Mrs. John, and you raised an unappeasable demon. The bump of self-esteem was well developed in her cranium. Mrs. John honestly believed that there was not a handsomer woman in St. Jude's county than herself, a better manager, nor one better educated. She had really been to a good school at St. Jude's for some years. She wrote a pretty hand, played some brilliant waltzes, and had read all through Enfield's Speaker; her English was decent. She wished her children to be educated, and also to be domesticated, and so some people might, I suppose, call her a good mother, but nobody would think her so who had lived a week with her in the house.

If the children dirtied their best frocks (which was the greatest crime they could commit in her eyes, because the destruction of property was the greatest of evils in her sight), she would beat them as savagely as Mr. Leslie leathered his boys; with this difference, that Leslie seemed rather to enjoy the administering of punishment, and was always serene, whereas Mrs. John was a perfect Hecate in her fury; her face would become quite demoniac in its expression, and the thumps and shakes and smacks *she* used to administer must have been really dangerous in their tendency. She was afraid of her husband, but of no other living mortal—not even Richard. She thought herself an elegant and refined person, whereas she was clumsy, ill-made, and heavy. She had had some money, and had therefore received some proposals, so she considered that she was, or at least had been fit for, the heroine of any of the love songs or love tales she had read. She had paid Kate Hall fifteen pounds a-year for instructing her little boy and girl, and she always considered it a great deal too much, although she insisted on Kate's cutting out and making all the children's dresses. At first she liked Miss Hall, because she was meek and humble, and afraid of *her*, and used to express admiration, unfeigned, for the beautiful silk dresses, velvet mantles, and gorgeous bonnets which Mrs. John kept hoarded in her trunks, until they became old-fashioned, or too small for her, or rather until she grew too large for them. But latterly Kate had ventured to cry at the quarrelling, and to shudder at the oaths, and even to remonstrate with the mother on her violence; and then Mrs. John arose in her wrath and called Miss Hall a canting, white-faced hypocrite, and made her pack up her things and leave at a moment's notice, and now woe betide poor Kate if Mrs. John should have it in her power to do her a damage, for she would assuredly do it in that case.

"I have brought Mr. Cruize home to dinner," said Richard to Mrs. John.

"I hope the turkey won't be spoilt," said Mrs. John, "that Martha is the most good-for-nothing hussey in the world;" wrath smouldered now in the sulky, black eye of Mrs. John. Martha had, indeed, been *getting* it with a vengeance.

"Take a seat, Mr. Cruize," in a rather civil tone to Martin, not *too* civil.

Mrs. John considered the schoolmaster very much beneath her, though, as a neighbour and one whom the men chose to bring in to smoke with them, he did very well of course, and Mr. Cruize took a seat and began to feel amused. She always amused him, he enjoyed the way in which she condescended to him, and the evident distance she deemed it right to maintain. She knew, of course, that Martin was poor, and she considered him, as she said, a respectable young man in his way.

While Martin was contrasting the house keeping of a Cumberland farmer, who dines on porridge, and has a new coat every seven years, with the profuse living or rather luxury of a midland country yeoman, Mrs. Richard came into the room. Mrs. Richard had no children; she was a very dressy person, she wore long gold ear rings, and her light hair was tied up with blue ribbons; she was very thin, her face was very white, she was very much better looking then Mrs. John, her expression, though sly, was sweeter; but that it might easily have been. She was considerably younger then Mrs. John; she too was very much afraid of her husband, she had two ruling passions, love of dress, and hatred of Mrs. John. She did not hoard her clothes as did her more stingy sister-in-law, but she did not go in so much for expense in rich material, so long as it was light, pretty and becoming, she did not care whether the fabric was silk or cotton.

"Let's ave in the turkey," said Richard.

"Where is Mr. John Higly?" asked Martin.

"He is gone into St. Jude's," said Mrs. John.

"Tell the wenches to send it in, can't you," said Richard to his wife.

So Mrs. Richard went into the kitchen, and

then tripped back, saying, with what was meant for a sweet smile, that the dinner was coming in.

"The wenches is after their sweethearts half the time," said Dick, "they wants good looking arter, and you're both too fine ladies to do it."

"Don't you talk in that way to me, if you please, Richard Higly," said Mrs. John, blazing up. "I hope I am not too fine to attend to my business. I may have good clothes, but I know how to take care of them. I hate fine ribbons messing about in a dairy, and dabbing into a gravy and messes. Ugh!" with a glance at little Mrs. Richard.

"Where's the yung uns?" said Dick.

"They've behaved most shamefully this morning," said Mrs. John; "they've spilt the cream all over the damask curtains in the parlour—I said they should have dry bread and water for their dinner, and I locked them up in their room, and there they shall stay till tea time."

Richard laughed.

"What a good mother you make! If I'd a yung un I'd rather send it to the workus ner trust it to you."

"It's to be hoped you'll never have any children," said Mrs. John.

"Well, I'm sure poor Jack's dosen't come off well."

Mrs. Richard laughed, and Mrs. John's stays crackled with wrath, and then the wenches brought in the hot turkey and sausages, and the great flagon was filled with cider, and the party sat down to eat. After the pudding was removed, Dick invited Martin to sit up to the fire and to fill his pipe; and he asked him to take a glass of brandy, but Martin said:—

"No, he never drank brandy."

"Whiskey?"

"No."

The two wives of drunken husbands thought well of Martin at that moment, but Richard said "bother," or a stronger word, and added that it was all trash.

"But we'll have some more cider," said he.

And he took out the flagon to get it replenished, and then he wickedly put into it nearly a quart of strong whiskey. With this he returned, and filled Martin's glass, and asked him to say if that was not a stronger tap than the last; and Martin, habitually temperate, and knowing little of the taste of liquors, never discovered the fraud. He drank half a glass of what he thought was simply very strong cider; it began to mount to his head, the stone hall swam before him, and the doors and windows changed places.

Richard began to jeer him a little, the ladies had gone about their household occupations, so the two sat alone.

"Can't thee stand a common drop of cider? ye must be as weak in th'ed as a child."

Martin felt a little annoyed at the hoarse laugh which followed this remark.

"I never tasted such strong cider in my life," said he.

Hereupon Richard re-filled his half-empty glass.

"Drink that up," said he, "it will do ye good, the best way is to take more drink if a little gets in your 'ed, it will steady ye; look ye here."

And he filled his own glass with the mixed stuff, and drained it to the dregs; it was mere child's play to him.

"No more, thank you," said Martin drowsily.

And he turned from his glass; but Richard was not going to let him escape so easily.

"It's pothering in that there school as makes a man weak, and no better nor an old woman," said he. "Oh, Lord, to think as a chap can't drink one glass of cider!!"

And Richard said some other things low, and almost insulting, and Martin, already stupified by the liquor, began to fancy that peace and release from Richard's jokes and importunity would be well purchased by compliance, and was weak enough to raise the glass and almost drain it. His hand shook so after that he could not find the table, and the glass fell, shivered to atoms, on the flagged floor. Then Richard was almost contented, only he wanted some witnesses to enjoy the sport.

"How is't now?" he asked, with a grin.

Martin felt ill, in fact, and unable to answer —the spirit had not the effect of exciting him, but of reducing his system, and completely stupefying him.

"I want," he said, "to lie down; I feel very ill."

And then, through the mists of drunkenness, which gathered thickly before his eyes, he saw the grin of Richard, and heard his rude laugh. In fine, Richard had his wish, for Martin was not able to sit up any longer, and so Richard rolled him down on the floor, and there Martin lay, helpless as a log of wood, with his head on a footstool, his eyes closed, his senses gone; Richard had reduced the intelligent man to a condition below that of a brute, and he was satisfied.

Just before six o'clock there came a rapping at the front door. One of "the wenches" opened it, the sound of an educated voice was heard in the passage, and the next moment there entered the Rev. F. Yardly, come to solicit the subscription of Mrs. John to aid in the sending out missionaries to Timbuctoo. The Higly's never gave away at the door, and very little did they give at any time, but considering Mr. Yardly's position and wealth, they deemed it right to treat him with respect to his face, and he seldom left their door without a half-crown.

"Good evening, Mr. Richard; is Mrs. John Higly in, and your wife?"

He had not noticed Martin yet.

"Yes, Mr. Yardly, they's in," said Richard, offering the clergyman (whom he always called the parson) a chair.

"I want to solicit their aid in sending out

two missionaries to Africa," said Mr. Yardly, "we wish to christianise the savages there."

Had Mr. Yardly turned his attention to the christianising of some of the savages in his own parish, and among them the brothers Higly, it would have been quite as well as sending instructors to Timbuctoo.

"Well," said Richard, rubbing his hands through his hair, "I'll ask the Missus, and Jack's wife about it, if you'll wait a bit, Mr. Yardly."

Just then Mr. Yardly's eye fell upon the wretched Martin, who, half coiled under the table, lay in his drunken sleep, with the fire-light full upon his pale face.

"Why, bless my soul," said Mr. Yardly, "who's that?"

And Richard would not shield his guest, the fun was too great to be lost; he chuckled and answered:—

"'Tis somebody as you knows very well."

And Mr. Yardly approached and recognised the schoolmaster of Alton.

"Drunk?" inquired Mr. Yardly, in a hoarse whisper.

Richard nodded.

"How? what?" asked Mr. Yardly; "he came here drunk?"

Richard did not say yea or nay; he only grinned. Mrs. King had been as good as her word; she had been up to Mr. Yardly, and poured her complaints into his ear within an hour of Martin's leaving the cottage. She had said a great deal about a love letter and Ella Thorpe, and Mr. Yardly had quite made up his mind to call upon Mrs. Thorpe, and tell her that Martin was an improper instructor for Ella, when the sight of him in a bestial state of drunkenness confirmed his worst suspicions, and made him give ready credence to all Mrs. King's tales about the public house, none of which were the least true.

"Nothing," said Mr. Yardly, "can compel me to keep that reprobate in the school till March, he shall never enter it again;"

then Richard felt a little qualm, not of conscience, but a fear of Martin's vengeance.

"He bean't often a drunken chap," he muttered, but he would not take the blame where it was due to himself, and confess that he alone was in fault.

"Rapscallion! rascal! villain!" said Mr. Yardly, who had never forgiven Martin's cool independence, "rapscallion! reprobate, he leaves Alton to-morrow."

Just then Mrs. John bustled into the kitchen, and was, or professed to be, horrified at Martin's condition, though so often had she seen her husband and brother-in-law in a much worse one, we can hardly believe in the reality of her emotion.

"We cannot be blamed, Mr. Yardly," said she, "for every one that Mr. Richard brings into the house. We're too liberal, that's the fault with us. I'm sure you can't be more shocked than I am, at finding that fellow under the table. Ugh! the nasty brute, he shall go if I turn him into the barn," and she was going out to call some farm servants to enforce her orders.

Richard put his hand upon hers, and said authoritatively but quietly, because of the parson:

"Let un bide."

So she let him bide, and Mr. Yardly continued to hold up his hands, and close his eyes, and denounce the vengeance of Heaven upon the wretched sinner under the table.

"If there were a pillory or a pair of stocks in the village," said Mr. Yardly, "he ought to be placed there; he shall be punished in some way. He shall be publicly disgraced, on that I am resolved."

"Won't you taste our cider, Mr Yardly?" asked Dick, "it's fine," and he prepared to leave the room.

Mr. Yardly was thirsty, Mr. Yardly liked cider; the Higly's were famed for their cider as for their cheese. Mr. Yardly knew this, and he said, "Yes, he would taste it," and

Richard brought him a jug full of pure clear cider, and the parson did more than taste it, he emptied two tumblers and was none the worse. But then Richard had played no trick upon him, and yet the beneficed clergyman holding up his hands, and closing his eyes, and almost anathemizing the schoolmaster, was as guilty as Martin, if guilt there be in drinking cider; only the one had to suffer for Richard Higly's fault, and the other had only his own sins to answer for.

"It's very good, very good in moderation," said the Vicar. "Thank you, Mrs. Higly," and he pocketed the half-crown for Timbuctoo; "but really what is to be done with this man to-night? I really cannot ask a respectable woman like Mrs. King to take him into her house." Oh, Charity! that suffereth long and is kind, how comes it about that many who profess to follow in His steps, who only breathed good will towards men, should know so little of thy Divine nature?

Mr. Yardly would have put Martin in the

stocks, was going to turn him adrift and breadless upon the world, and to disgrace him in the eyes of his compeers, and yet Mr. Yardly thought he was a pious man, walking straight towards the new Jerusalem, a candidate for the snowy robe, and the crown of gold, and the tuneful harp, those poetic metaphors which the inspired teachers of old held out towards the first striving suffering christians. Mr. Yardly, fat, comfortable, rich, honoured, was not exactly what I should term a struggling christian; he never, I believe, had any inward struggles — why should he? He believed honestly that he was all right, and he quite thought that he did his duty in denouncing and punishing Martin to the utmost; and perhaps he did, only I would feign think that we, who stand so much in need of pardon, must needs be lenient one towards another—"As we forgive them that trespass against us." But Mr. Yardly liked better the quality of justice than of "Mercy;"

and here let us pause to reflect for an instant what a very short-sighted thing our justice is sometimes. Mr. Yardly's justice, to wit, was most unjust, if I may be allowed the paradoxical expression. He was ignorant of the true facts of the case, he denounced Martin, whose fault was inadvertence, and he spoke fair words to Richard, the habitual drunkard, Richard, whose almost devilish cunning was the sole cause of Martin's condition.

At last he left the Higlys, expressing great pity for Mrs. John, and advising them all not to let Martin sleep in the house.

"You should not encourage drunkenness, Mrs. Higly," he said.

When he was gone Mrs. John accused Richard of mixing spirits in the cider. Richard laughed, and did not deny it. Mrs. John, who seldom lost an opportunity of scolding, now began to rate her brother-in-law soundly.

"You see if it doesn't get about," she said;

"you see if the young fellow doesn't suspect something to-morrow, and then won't John be mad?"

Just at this juncture they heard the voice of Mr. John in the yard, calling to a man to take his horse, and the next moment he walked into the room. He was astonishingly like Richard, with blotched face and swelled nose, he wore top boots and a riding coat.

"What's thee been up to?" said he to Mrs. John.

Oh, how she was cowed when he spoke, she was silent at once, and let Richard and his wife point to Martin and tell the tale. John laughed, sat down, and began to draw off his boot.

"And did the parson bide here long?" he asked.

"About half-an-hour, ur it might be three quarters," said Dick.

"Did ye mix any whiskey in the parson's cider?" asked John, whereupon they all laughed, and Dick said—

"No;" and John said—

"If I'd a bin here, I'd a put some in the parson's, while my hand was in. Set the tea," to his wife, and Mrs. John set the tea, and Mrs. Richard made some buttered toast, and the wench brought in the lamp, and the light fell full upon the white face of the luckless Martin, who stirred, and moaned a little.

"He looks very ill," said Mrs. Richard, "hadn't we better get him to bed?"

"Bed," cried Mrs. John, "do you think I'm going to spoil my best bed, by putting such a fellow into it as that?"

"Let un bide," said John, "where a is." So they let un bide, and then suddenly Mr. John said—"Where's the yung uns?"

Mrs. John explained.

Whereupon Mr. John in language more remarkable for strength than elegance, ordered her to bring them down, and soon after a little purple girl, and a little yellow boy, dressed in linsey frocks, and large pinafores, (Mrs. John was not ambitious in regard to the toilette of her children) appeared on the scene; they had thick straight hair cut in crops over their foreheads, the girl was purple from cold, the boy was yellow by nature; they both looked frightened, as well they might, with such a mother as Mrs. John; these children were densely stupid, and what wits they had Mrs. John frightened out of them.

"Well, Jack," said the father to his namesake, "has thee bin spilling crame on the curtains?"

Jack hung his head.

"If ever they dare to so much as look inside the parlour again," said Mrs. John, "I'll cut them in pieces," and Mrs. John looked quite capable of carrying out her threat. Our hanging laws are really useful in some degree, inasmuch as they *do* restrain some violent hands from hasty deeds, I am confident.

Then began the business of tea and toast, and it happened that Martin began to awaken now to a dim perception of his situation, and even to understand a part of what was going on around him.

"He'll be turned out, that's certain," said Mrs. Richard, "the parson's determined on that. I'm sorry for him, poor fellow, he's but young."

"He would'nt thank Dick, if he knew what he mixed in the cider," said Mrs. John.

"It's a pity but what he'd gived the parson some too," said John, "cider's a liquor as the parson's very fond on, he'd a drunk a quart as easy as pap."

"Richard would have had that to answer for," said Mrs. John, and Richard grinned, and said—

"I know'd that afore," and he winked slyly, and all this Martin saw and heard from his place, under the table, and yet he *felt* totally unable to move; something like wild but undefined rage towards Richard Higly stirred at his heart, but as yet he hardly appreciated his situation.

"Richard know'd as 'twas no good to trick the parson," continued John Higly, "but if I'd a bin here I'd a done it."

"I'll warrant the parson is as fond of a drain a spirits as we are," said Richard, "if a can get u.n on the sly?"

"Ay, I'll warrant him," said John. "How much didst thee put in the schoolmaster's?"

"Nigh on a quart in the big flagon, but a dident drink but a tumbler and a half mixed with cider, he's like one of the yung uns in the head or worse."

"Never tasted it before, poor fellow, in his life," said Mrs. John, contemptuously.

Martin's senses were returning to him, he had quite understood the last remarks; his head now ached fearfully, but the spirit had not made him feel sick, nor excited him, it had only thrown him into a stupor, and from this he was fast awakening. He listened hard. For the next quarter of an hour, he only heard the market prices discussed, and saw John take out a dirty leather bag, and count over one hundred sovereigns in his hands, the price of some pigs he had sold, then he tied them up again. Mrs. John was requested to put on the spirits and water, and Mrs. Richard cleared away the tea things because "the wenches" were milking.

Mrs. John and Mrs. Richard had been to school, each was the daughter of a rich St. Jude's county farmer;—the girls of the farming families in that country are nearly always sent to a boarding school for three or four years, but the boys are usually taught by the village schoolmaster to write and cast-up accounts, and here their education ends if they are to be brought up to the farming, and they nearly all speak in the broad country dialect; so that if you go into a farm-house you will not be at all unlikely to find the daughters playing overtures on an expensive piano, and able to tell you in what year Sir Walter Scott died and what were his principal works, while the sons know little beyond the farming interests and the county gossip, and discuss these in an accent so broad as to be all but unintelligible to a stranger.

Martin was not ruminating on these particulars, he was devising a plan of vengeance, open and summary, on Richard Higly; he was however, too weak to put it into practice. An overwhelming sense of shame and degradation oppressed him, for in these days, Heaven be thanked, intemperance is not the rule but the exception, and nearly all the young men of the present time are ashamed of a fit of drunkenness. Of course, Martin thought of Ella and felt as though he were unfit to stand in her presence, and imagined that she would indeed loathe him if the knowledge of his weakness reached her; because when a man really loves a woman he nearly always exalts her into an angel of purity and refinement. Ella was more of an imp than an angel; she would have laughed heartily at Richard's trick and Martin's state, she would have thought none the worse of him for it; indeed had her name been Harry Thorpe instead of Ella, there is every chance that she would have played the self-same trick off on somebody herself.

Martin at last came from under the table, and staggered to his feet. A roar of laughter greeted him.

"Where've thee bin to, Master Cruize?" said Richard.

Now who can be dignified under circumstances like these in which Martin found himself placed? Martin never attempted it; he took the first chair that offered, and said, putting his hand to his head,

"Will you kindly let me have a cup of strong coffee?"

He had heard something about strong coffee being good for complaints like that he was suffering from.

Mrs. John, who now understood that the Vicar was about to dismiss the young man, and that he was miserably poor, resolved to insult him on the "Hit him hard, he's got no friends," principle.

"Here, Jane," she called to one of the wenches, "bring this man a cup of coffee; he's been very drunk."

Martin opened his eyes stupidly upon Mrs. John, and wondered what she was up to; however, when the coffee came he drank it up, and his head was infinitely better after it.

"You should mind what you drink," said Mrs. John, "you can't expect to do the same as those that have been used to good living like Mr. Higly."

Mrs. John had no spite against Martin, but she liked having somebody to scold, and to put down; the children were in bed, and the schoolmaster did as well as anybody else.

"I am very much obliged for your advice," said Martin, who, perfectly aware of the trick which had been practised upon him, was burning with inward wrath.

"You need not be obliged to me," said Mrs. John. "I think, my young man, you hardly know your place; you seem to forget who you are talking to."

"Who am I talking to?" said Martin.

"You low, impudent fellow," said Mrs. John, furiously, "you'll find yourself turned out to-morrow without a character, and *then* see if your saucy tongue will serve you."

Then John Higly turned upon his wife.

"Thee hold thine," he said. "Thine is the sharpest (and another word which we omit) tongue in the country. Some day I'll make thee bite it through."

Mrs. John scowled, and walked out of the room.

The knocker was pounded against the front door, and in another moment Mr. Clyne, the curate, entered. He removed his hat, and asked gently to see Mr. Cruize? What a halo there is round *real* goodness and worth? The meek head of the curate, which (tonsure excepted) might have served as a "study" for Sterne's monk of the order of St. Francis, seemed something Divine among those blotched faces and hardened eyes and low brows of the Higlys; and even Martin, powerful as was his countenance, appeared a being of a lower grade than Robert Clyne, for his face was sad and heavy. The curate, with a smile of love and kindness, with large, clear, spiritual eyes bent pityingly upon the schoolmaster, looked almost like a good angel.

"I want you to come home to my house, Martin," said the poor Curate, "I have a bed."

"Thank you," said Martin.

"Won't yer sit down?" said John Higly, pushing a chair towards Mr. Clyne.

He sat down, and thanked John Higly.

"Are you not ready to come yet, Martin."

"I am quite ready," said Martin, turning away his face and lowering his eyes, "quite ready."

Mrs. John flounced in, carrying the great flagon full of cider. She put it on the table, and shook hands condescendingly with the poor curate.

"Will you taste our cider, Mr. Clyne."

"Not any, thank you."

"Dear me, I suppose you're a teetotaller, then," said Mrs. John, "I think such ways are foolish; I call it despising God's good gifts."

"I hope not that," said the Curate, "cider and wine, and all strong drinks are useful and pleasant, I admit—"

"Ah, perhaps you don't like it?"

"Yes, I like it, but I have accustomed myself to do without them."

"Ah, I suppose for a sort of penance, like the Roman Catholics, self denial, I suppose," and she laughed rather contemptuously.

"No," said the Curate, smiling, "you have not hit upon my reason yet, Mrs. Higly."

"Like enough he saves the money it would cost un," said Richard, "and that ud make some difference in a curate's pay."

"Yes, Mr. Higly, you have guessed wisely. It is to *save* that I abstain from everything strong."

"Well, when people are poor, they must

cut their coat according to their cloth, of course," said Mrs. John, throwing some coals on the fire.

The Curate rose now to take his leave, and Martin rose also, but the latter spoke no word to any of the Higlys; he walked out of the place and into the passage; they burst into a roar of laughter.

"He's offended," said John, winking at the Curate. "A got drunk, and t'other parson comed in and found un; he do like to make a bit of a row, and a says a'll turn him off to-morrow."

"I am afraid he will," said Mr. Clyne, "he called upon me and said so."

"Well," said Richard, filling his pipe, "a hadn't ought to a got drunk, a ought to follow you, Mr. Clyne, and save the money, as he ain't strong enough to stand liquors."

"It is the first time such a thing has happened to him since he has been here, and so I told Yardly, but it was no use whatever. Good night, Mr. Higly," he shook hands with them all, and followed Martin out into the passage; they pulled back the door, and stepped out into the wild winter night—the bitter wind was tearing and howling about them, and as they began to cross the fields, the heavy gusts blew into their faces, and prevented anything like regular conversation; there were showers, too, of hard pelting rain every other ten minutes, and the heavens were clouded so, that for some time the stars were completely hidden; when they emerged into the village, some of these black clouds rolled away, however, and the grey blue sky, set thickly with stars, was over their heads.

"It looks like hope," said the Curate, pointing upwards.

Martin answered never a word; so they pursued their way in silence until they reached the Curate's lodgings. Here they ascended the stairs rapidly, and the Curate stirred his fire into a blaze, then when he turned his head after he found that Martin had sunk upon the floor, that his face was buried in his hands on the sofa, and that he seemed given up to an abandonment of grief. Mr. Clyne went up to him.

"My dear friend," said he, tenderly.

Martin answered by a convulsive sob.

"You are ill," said the good Curate.

"No, no, Mr. Clyne, don't talk to me, don't pity me, I am a cursed wretch, it is no use to help me, I have been drunk, reduced to the level of an animal; I am degraded in my own eyes, but it was not my fault, it was not indeed; that brute, Dick Higly—"

"It is no use now to be angry with him, or with yourself, Martin, the future is all you have to think of; never, never take more than your head can stand again."

"I only had a glass and a half."

"My dear Martin, you mistake.

"No, that devil Higly put whisky in the flagon. I heard him joke about it, when I was coming to myself under the table; his brother asked him why he had not put some into Mr. Yardly's glass also, and he admitted that he should have been afraid; but I feel just as degraded as if I had known, and done it with my eyes open; the 'Thorpes.'"

"I will make it all right with them."

"I'll thrash Dick Higly," said Martin, slowly.

"No, you won't, Martin."

"I will."

"You know," said the Curate, "that the old proberb says 'To err is human, to forgive divine.'"

"I don't want to be divine, I am satisfied to be human. I feel something worse now, like a demon."

"Does your head ache?"

"Oh, I wish it would ache until it drove me raving mad; then I could forget my misery."

"Now, look here, dear impatient Martin; it is true that Mr. Yardly is going to turn you away from the school, but he cannot take away your capabilities and talents; why should you not advertise for a situation as usher in a school, for instance? you could get it at once; refer your applicants to me, and until then I will share what I have with you, you can stay here."

"Dear, good, noble, generous," said Martin, breaking down; "you are almost enough to reconcile me to this cant they call religion. Yardly called on you, did he?"

"Oh, yes," said the Curate, sorrowfully, "he seemed quite cut up about it."

"Poor man," said Martin, scornfully, "one thing is, he is a fool, so I forgive him."

"And poor Richard Higly," said the Curate mildly, "is not a very wise man, won't you forgive him?"

"No, I shall thrash him," said Martin, through his clenched teeth. "I shall strike Dick Higly with a hunting whip."

"Mr. Yardly said that—that—"and the

Curate hesitated, "Mrs. King would not receive you again."

"What she!" said Martin, "poor old soul, I am afraid I was very rude to her—called her an idiot, or something; I only owe her about seven shillings now though, which I will pay her to-morrow."

"And Mr. Yardly owes *you* nothing?" asked the Curate.

"No, only I think, as he turns me away on so short a notice, he ought to pay me something. I wish Leslie could pay me;" and the troubled, perplexed look which anxiety about money brings, came into Martin's face.

"To-morrow you must see about all that. Now you had better get to bed. I brought up your little dressing box from Mrs. King's, the rest of the things you can get in the morning," and the curate took Martin into his neat little bed-room, and then he went to bed, and even to sleep.

Thus we have seen each in the exercise of what he considered his christian duty, both the *vicar* and the curate, and it depends upon the reader's own judgment to decide whether the orthodox believer in the terrors of the law, or the eccentric intrepreter of the letter of the new testament was in the right.

CHAPTER IX.

DISGRACED.

"AND I can only regret, Mr. Clyne, that you should harbour in your house a person of known bad character, a dissipated sinner, whom I feel it to be my bounden duty to hunt out of the village before he corrupts the boys committed to his charge; it is not well for a clergyman of the church of England to protect every villain that applies to him. I am seriously displeased with your conduct in this matter, Mr. Clyne—you really must excuse my saying so."

Mr. Clyne was obliged to excuse the vicar

in any case, whatever he might think proper to say to him; he stood very meekly in his little parlour listening to the reproof of his elder in the church, who had called upon him to reprimand him thus severely.

"And where is that fellow now?"

"He is in bed," said the curate, timidly, "his head ached so, he could not get up."

"Faugh!" The vicar's disgust was overpowering. "And really, Mr. Clyne, do I understand that you countenance this proceeding? do you think this is drunkenness" —'under extenuating circumstances,' the vicar might have said, that was what he meant, but he would have thought any illusion to French trials, or any newspaper but "the Record," sacrilegious. "Do you think this drunkenness that may be pardoned, because the weather is cold, or anything of that sort?"

"No, I consider drunkenness under any circumstances very sinful."

"Then you admit that you harbour in your house a great sinner?"

"But surely, Mr. Yardly, our Saviour did not turn away from sinners—*where* should *we* all be if he had?"

"You cannot form deductions in that absurd manner, Mr. Clyne; *you* cannot pardon or cleanse a lost sinner. You can only do your duty as a Master, Pastor and Instructor, scourging the wicked and separating them from your flock, pointing out the awfulness of sin, and expressing your deep horror of it. You know David says, 'I will not know a wicked person,' neither should a christian; but you, Mr. Clyne, it seems, have positively been on intimate terms with this reprobate, Martin Cruize!"

"Martin Cruize is not a reprobate, Mr. Yardly—he never was drunk before last night, and there was whiskey in his cider which he did not know of."

"Lies," said Mr. Yardly, "horrible lies

added to his other sins. Mr. Clyne, I am astonished at your weakness. You are *not* a valiant soldier putting on the armour of righteousness, and fighting the good fight manfully, but a feeble renegade, having a part with the sinners. No, the more I think of it the more am I shocked at it," said Mr. Yardly; "I can only beg, nay, insist on your turning this young man out of your lodgings at once; if not, my course towards you will be very decided, I assure you."

The curate knew that the vicar had no power to punish him for entertaining a person like Martin, who had not infringed and was not amenable to the laws; and that his threat was merely the bravado of a man who liked power, and punishing others very much; but still he did not wish to offend or annoy Mr. Yardly, and so he formed a plan for the accommodation of the schoolmaster which should not insult the prejudices of the vicar.

"He will go, Mr. Yardly, when he awakes," he said. "But I must say, that I think, nay, I am certain that the conduct you consider right to pursue towards the schoolmaster, is exactly contrary to the spirit of the gospel, and do not think that I mean to desert Mr. Cruize; I tell you frankly, I shall look narrowly after his interest."

"I hope you will not do that openly, it would be such a terrible example to set—the vicar of the parish dismisses a servant for drunkenness, and the curate receives that stinging viper into his bosom, and looks after his interest. You are not, perhaps, aware, Mr. Clyne, what a proud, impertinent, insubordinate fellow that schoolmaster is; you do him a great injury instead of a kindness in helping him to another employ, it would do him infinite service to be cast on the world without a character and without a situation, it would bring down his rebellious spirit."

"And in this bitter weather he might die of hunger and cold," said the curate, sadly.

"Oh, you talk wildly, Mr. Clyne—die, indeed, I am sure a little hunger and cold would be the best discipline that bad young man could have. You know, you must know, that he is a godless sinner; he reads novels, I have caught him reading works of fiction last summer, do you approve of that—would you waste your time so?"

"No, because I have no time to waste, and I find enough, and too much field for my sympathies in the sorrows of real humanity without going to fiction."

"And yet you make this low trifler your friend; besides, Mr. Clyne, one must act up to the position in life in which it has pleased God to place one. You are a clergyman, and a gentleman, this man is only the village schoolmaster."

"It is a part of my policy to make no distinctions of rank."

"Then let me tell you, sir," said the vicar, waxing red, "let me tell you, that you are not fit for a clergyman. You ought not to have entered the church with these loose notions."

"Perhaps not," replied the curate, "I certainly seem to cause my Vicar a great deal of pain, but what can I do? Oh, how hard it is to do right," and he sighed. Mr. Yardly was not a bit touched by the Curate's meekness, nor pleased at his self-devotion and nobleness; he was not a man to be touched by anything fine in human nature; to him the whole creation were groveling in wickedness, except the choice few, who thought as he did.

"And how could you possibly sleep last night?" said the Vicar, "your bed is very small."

"I did not go to bed," said the Curate, hastily.

The Vicar's lip curled with disdain. "You did sacrifice yourself; I hope you employed your time well, in reading good things, or in composing a sermon?"

"I did not remain in the house."

Mr. Yardly looked at him with severity stamped upon every feature.

"Then, Mr. Clyne, as your vicar, I have a

right to ask you where did you pass the night?"

Those clear innocent eyes of Robert Clyne looked almost with the simple wonder of a child into the Vicar's face, as he answered—

"In old Kite's Cottage, he is one of Squire Alton's tenants, you know, and his wife is very ill. I thought she was dying, and she has been afraid to die, and has not slept for nights. I was there reading, and trying to make her believe. She was an infidel when I first came here. Now she believes in God, and I am trying to bring her to a still more saving faith."

"Sad people, sad people those," said the Vicar, "always impudent, and saucy, even when half-starving. Has Kite work?"

"Very little, he can't earn much."

The truth was the Curate half-supported these people, and this the Vicar had been told one day by old Kite himself.

"You seem to make quite favorites of the Kites, Mr. Clyne?"

"Not at all, if I allowed human prejudice to sway me I fancy I should find little charity or interest in my heart for poor Mrs. Kite. One is so weak, so moved by exteriors and manner."

"But you willingly spent a whole night in that cold, dirty hole; either your self-denial is extraordinary, or the Kites are favourites," and the Vicar looked with contempt at the good young Curate.

Just then the door between the two rooms opened, and Martin, looking very pale, but perfectly neat and respectable, walked into the room.

"That partition is so thin," said he, "that I have overheard all your conversation while dressing."

The Vicar was purple with anger and surprise.

"You have heard me say, then, what I repeat now, I dismiss you at once. Mr. Clyne is my witness. I have disgraced you thoroughly in Alton this day. I have told the parents of several of the scholars that, when school recommences, there will be another master. I have called on Mrs. Thorpe, and told of your sending a letter to her daughter; she has utterly forbidden her daughter to speak to you again."

Martin grew livid.

"Do you dare to call yourself a christian?" he said furiously, and now, feeling that all was lost, not attempting to control the vehemence of his passion, "you are a hard-hearted, selfish, tyrannical, purse-proud priest, with no claim to any other feeling than contempt; for every charge that you bring against me, I will bring ten against you."

"Am I a drunkard?"

"You are a mischief-maker, a tale-bearer, a grasping sinner, thinking only how you may best add house to house, and field to field. Why were you not at your post last night, praying in cold hovels by the bed-side of dying paupers? Your interpretation of a priest's duties is this—'I will fare sumptuously every day. I will clothe myself in purple and fine linen, and let the beggars lie at my gates full of sores, the dogs may lick them if they like. This good, pure, patient man is your dog, who goes out to heal the vexed and wounded, but I could carry on my simile farther, and see you at the end of the parable 'tormented in this flame.' Take care that the hell you prophesy for others is not your own portion. I mean remorse—remorse, Francis Yardly, for duties neglected, orphans unfed, that your bounty might have cherished; widows' hearts left desolate that you might have made to sing for joy."

And Martin, the accused, the disgraced, the ruined, looked almost sublime in his pale wrath, as he stood in fearless denunciation of his superior, pointing the finger of scorn at him, and with a lip curled by disdain, and a certain pride; much of this was hate and vengeance, for the wrong Yardly had done him in Ella's eyes, but neither of the clergymen knew this; the Vicar could not believe his ears, he had expected to find Martin sullen, but crouching and frightened, and now he *found* him turned accuser, and so Mr. Yardly held his tongue, because he knew that he *could* do no more to Martin than send him out penniless, and characterless; this he had threatened to do, and meant to do, and Martin knew it, and dared him to do his worst, and was most emphatically ready to render him railing for railing.

So he turned to the Curate—

"Mr. Clyne, until that ruffian is out of the village, I do not consider myself safe. Pray remember that."

And the Vicar ignominiously retreated, leaving Martin master of the field.

CHAPTER X.

THE LAST LOOK.

Martin was to leave Alton, with no character, and with precisely one pound nine and seven-pence in his pocket. Martin was to go out into the world to begin life anew,—or what is called life,—that droning, joyless existence, that seems hardly worth having unless we can raise our eyes beyond the grey dull present, to a time when, if we faint not, it is promised to us that our joy shall be full. But these promises were nought to Martin Cruize, he looked steadily into his dreary future with a dogged resolve that had taken the place of his sometime patience; he was bitter to his heart's core, because life had become so bitter to him. He never forgot his oath. Ella was his wife, and sooner or later he would claim her, and tear her by force from her family, if he could obtain her in no other way, but first he would strive to win bread and a home for her. How? oh, the bitterness of the empty echo that answered him, reverberating to his soul with throes of anguish. How? poor, despised, cast out beggar! How? struggling teacher of dead languages! How, in that great teeming Babel, which you are about to enter, can you turn your poor acquirements to account? Who wants your instruction, who would give two shillings for your knowledge? Make way, make way, for the busy, thriving man of the world, to aid whose progress the crowd parts asunder, and who is climbing with hasty steps the hill of fame. Your place is on the ground, down in the dirt, *there* let the multitude trample you in the dust, and crush out your heart against the stones.

To some of us this mocking fiend has spoken words as cruel as those it whispered to the schoolmaster. Martin let the demon babble on, he was sitting before the curate's fire, it was night. The next day he was to start to London, his eyes were fixed abstractedly upon the blaze, the curtains were drawn, the candles were not lighted, his little trunk was packed in the next room, his little bills were paid, (Leslie had not paid him) he was going into a small lodging recommended to him by Mr. Clyne, he was to advertise in "The Times," for daily tuitions, or for an engagement as private tutor. If he had not loved and desperately, he would have looked more hopefully at his prospects, but his heart was gnawed upon by a most devouring passion; the woman he loved was his unclaimed, unloving, unconscious wife, and how dared he dream of breaking to her the astounding truth.

He *did* dream of it lately; she had been very kind to him, true she had nothing else to amuse her now, that that old reprobate lay in the house. He understood now the reason of her mad marriage, but still she *was* kind, she looked kind. "Fool, dolt, idiot," said the demon, "she is only mocking you, she has no heart, that woman. Look how she has voluntarily condemned herself to a single unloved life, she has no natural affections nor passions, she lives for excitement alone, and pleasure; can you give her these? Can you provide her with an opera box, and fast horses, and grand balls; she would spit in your face if you told her she was your wife, she would trample your love to the earth. "But I will earn enough to give her all she needs," said Martin. "You may perhaps manage to gain twenty pounds a year, and your board," said the fiend, "after first waiting and starving a time; perhaps you can allow her half of that salary, or will you both keep a day school together at five shillings a quarter per head?" "If she begs in the streets with me, she shall come at last," swore Martin, furiously.

"Certainly, if you can persuade her to that, but it strikes me that she is a lady who will have her own way; besides where is your honour? You have spent her hundred pounds." "Though I had spent ten thousand, though my honour were shattered till I became a thief, a house-breaker, a galley slave, still is Ella my wife, still mine, my own."

"As for becoming a galley slave," said the fiend, "there is no reason you should not. Your passions are hot as hell; your purse is empty, and you have no friends."

Martin gnashed his teeth, and stamped his feet, when the demon spoke thus. How was he to win bread, not for himself, but for her? And like lightning a thought darted across his brain, why should he not *write?*

Ah! how many have taken that thought to their hearts, and cherished it fondly like a hope of golden promise, why not? why not, as well as others? and the poor deluded aspirant has gone on working and hoping, and writing, fondly clothing his ideas in chosen words, and reading and re-reading his manuscript with beating heart. What if these written thoughts should resound through the world, what if the echoes of *my* fame, *mine* should boom from afar? What if gold should pour in, and honour, and happiness? And then come the long months of waiting, the sickening deferred hope, the refusal of the publishers, or if printed "the crushing sarcasms of the press."

The question is gaily and jauntily put, why waste good paper by printing on it such type? and the ignorance of the author is pleasantly sneered at, *he* who did not know what good society was, why attempt to paint it? and sometimes the caustic words come painfully home to the wretched writer. He who wrote in a garret, and could not pay for his coals, what should he know about gallant gentlemen, and laughing ladies in silken drawing-rooms? He drew on his imagination, alas! and thus he was laughed at. If he had written of what he knew of, his garret? his hunger? his wild misery? his dull hopeless life? would the press have been more favourable? who can say? And all this is right and just; if there were no "Saturday *refiner*," no most "*Erudite Regarder*," to laugh down the weaknesses and ignorance of us scribblers, would not the world be more hopelessly inundated than it is even with our lucubrations? If the "Erudite Regarder" did not tell me that my characters were waxen figures, I might produce worse inanities than I do even, but some pity, gentle reader, is craved by the struggling author, who strives so hard to please you and whose heavy heart the stinging words of the "Erudite Regarder" wound horribly. So Martin would write, the thought was so sunny that, abashed at its light, the mocking fiend fled away howling, and Martin sat with a glow upon his cheek, and a fire in his eye, scheming, plotting. What should he write?

Poetry, he had written some hasty rhymes in the past summer, before he had known that he loved Ella; the thoughts had suggested themselves after a stroll through the cloisters of St. Jude's, and a survey of an old Prebendal Mansion, which stood in the meadow on the other side of the river; he went to his trunk, unfastened it, and rummaged for his papers. Of course he could write much better things than *that*, still he would have a look at the silly rhymes by the fire light; he knelt down, conned them over, felt very justly ashamed of them, and thought of putting them in the flames. Clatter, clatter, down the village street, tramp, tramp, nearer and nearer, comes the sound of a horse's hoofs at full gallop. Sometimes there is an instinct comes to us with a sound. We know that a hand and a voice, and a throbbing life are near us, which are dear and precious, and adorable in our eyes. Martin threw the papers on the floor, and listened; nearer and nearer came the hoof's clatter, trotting at a mad flying pace. Nobody ever rode so fast as Ella, no horse had such a sounding hoof as Black Fan. He knew both; but at eight o'clock at night, Ella out riding! he went to the window, he heard a musical voice say gaily to a passer by: "Will you kindly hold my horse?" The next moment, that little knocker was struck against the door.

Could Ella be come on a message to the curate about the dying old sinner at the court? he would fain hope not on such an errand, because he heard her gay laugh, as the door was opened; the next moment she had bounded up the stairs, and stood beside him in the flickering fire-light, dressed in habit, jaunty hat, and feather.

"Hollo!" said she; "down in the dumps?"

"Miss Thorpe, take a chair?"

"Not if I know it. I'm not going to stop here long, because Black Fan won't wait. I've been out to Cremorne Court, spent the day there, and I've sent John home another way. I said I had some places to call at, some poor people to see. I meant you, I heard you were here, and were turned off, and drunk, and not to come again, and what not, and I resolved to find out the truth from you. So you and Brimstone have been going on any how, I hear; do tell me all about it. Speak up!" and she laid her riding whip playfully across his shoulders. Martin was in no playful mood; he could scarcely remember the common usages of politeness, he remained where he was standing near the fire place without attempting to obey Ella, and "speak up;" that fastest of fast girls continued to ply him with questions:

"Were you not really drunk, though?"

"Yes, dead drunk, and under the table, unable to speak or move!"

"Oh, old Brimstone was right, then," said Ella, in a disappointed tone. "I thought he'd been telling lies again."

"I don't think he exactly tells lies," said Martin.

"Then you mean that you deserve to be

turned off, and Brimstone is in the right, after all ?"

"Brimstone, as you call him, is a hard, cruel, harsh man. I don't deserve to be turned off at all," and then Martin told Ella of Dick Higly, and the mixing of whiskey, and also of the plain speaking he had given to the vicar.

She clapped her hands. "And did you really tell him he was purse-proud, and harsh? how good, how excellent. Let me tell you, Mr. Cruize, you are a brick !"

"Thank you, Miss Thorpe, that is high praise from you.

"Of course it is. I don't know whether the genus brick has not more charms for me even than the genus darling. I say, Mr. Cruize, I wish you were a gentleman."

"Thank you," said Martin, turning hot all over.

"Don't thank me; what I've said sounds insulting, when that is the last thing on earth I mean to be to you. You see I only mean I wish the world recognised you as my equal, *for you are my equal quite*, if not my *superior*, eh?"

"Forget that," said Martin. "I was mad when I spoke those words."

"You were the very coldest and calmest madman, then, I ever heard of."

"Cold and calm, Miss Thorpe? Oh, GOD!"

"What on earth do you mean? don't act a —— scene here, my dear fellow; don't mistake me. I am a little, flirting, heartless minx, who have played sad pranks with you, I fear; yes, don't speak, I know it all—you're desperately in love with me. Ain't you? of course I know it, I should be a fool if I didn't, and at first I thought it high spree; cruel fun, a delicious joke. I felt awfully jolly about it."

"And now," gasped Martin.

"Now I'm awfully sorry."

"Why, tell me, why?'

Martin had approached her with a fierce,

eager face; he was hungering for her words, as a famished wolf might hunger for its prey:

"Why, tell me why?"

"Because your face is so dreadful; your great eyes look so full of something that I can't laugh at, that I feel pity. I'm sure you are in such deep earnest."

"Look here, Ella," said Martin. "Words would be weak as water to express one half of the great passion you have created in me; but I am poor, poor, with only a few, few shillings in the world. To-morrow I go to London to try and earn my bread by working my brains in some way. To urge such a suit as mine is the folly of a chained lunatic. I should not have spoken had you not told me that you knew my secret, but there it is, my burning, scorching secret is out. I have told you that I am a starving beggar, and that I worship you. Why don't you laugh at me?"

"Because I can't."

"Because you have some pity for me, but no love? Oh, Ella! say, have you no love?"

"Not a tittle. I am not flirting now, only speaking the plain truth. Not a particle, not because you are the schoolmaster of Alton, but because I have no affection to give to anybody."

"But some day you will have."

"Never," she said, firmly, "I did fancy I loved, but I found the man was a humbug; now I have taken a kind of vow never to marry, never to love."

Martin hoped again; it was the wild oaths on the altar steps that prevented her from softening, and that shut up her heart against him, nothing else.

"Then you tell me to think of you as one married," he said, pointedly.

She started, but restrained herself.

"If you like," she said; "or as of one dead, that is the more poetical way of putting it; and look here, Mr. Cruize, the sooner you get rid of those foolish fancies the better. Meanwhile take this five-pound note, which you refused before; do, do take it, it will comfort me to think that I have at least been of some help to one whom I have pained for my selfish pleasure."

Her voice shook a little, and Martin folded up her little offering in silence, and put it into his pocket.

"Thank you for doing it without making a fuss."

"I mean to thrash Dick Higly," said Martin; "he is the cause of my leaving Alton—Alton, the paradise of my soul—and I shall thrash him."

"Don't."

"Why not?"

"He will summons you; you will have to pay a fine; you will be doubly disgraced."

"But he ought to be punished, I wish him to know what I think of him."

"Will you leave him to me?"

"To you!"

"I will go down there on Fan, call him out,

and tell him what I think of him. I will tell him I saved him from a terrible thrashing, by persuading you to let him alone. I will say I think him a coward, a sneak, and see if I don't cover him with shame."

"But Mrs. John, his brother's wife?"

"Oh, she is a complete toady and humbug; she is the most servile woman I ever met. She thinks I'm a great heiress. Will you promise not to strike that wretched Dick?"

"I would promise *you* anything you asked, right or wrong."

"And now, old fellow, good bye; somehow I feel like crying at parting from you, our last half a dozen lessons have been so pleasant."

She put her gloved hand in his, he pressed it passionately.

"Good bye, good bye; there's Fan tearing and snorting. Good bye, I must go, don't be foolish."

She was gone, gone perhaps for ever, from his yearning, anxious arms, from his outraged heart, from his cheerless life; she was gone, his *wife*, and he sank down and groaned aloud.

That night he would not sleep in the Curate's bed, but said he would lie on the sofa; but in the dead of the night he arose and dressed, and slipped noiselessly out of the house, and made away for Alton Hall.

He was going to take a last look under the winter sky at the house which had been so much to him; he was going to watch the window which was Ella's, and there, unmindful of the keen wind, he was about to commune with his own thoughts, to look more calmly into his future, less regretfully into his past, more hopefully at his present. In a short time he had climbed the ha ha which separated the park from the road, he had skirted the shrubberies, and now he had cut across the grass, and stood confronting the half modern mansion.

The house itself seemed asleep. It was one of those times when the half moon sails swiftly upon the banks of dark clouds, when here and there a bright star peers out from the greyish distant sky, when the spirit of the night seems to be riding upon the wings of the wind, and a kind of *presence* is felt by the lonely watcher, who, bowed down by care or anxiety, or distracted by passion, leaves the land of sleep, where nature had purposed that his soul should bathe itself, and comes to look at the outer world in the solemn time of dreams. It was as though the very woods, whose nakedness was hidden by the night-shadows, were asleep, and dreaming—dreaming of green boughs and radiant blossoms, and of violets and primroses clustering about their feet; it was as though the little lake dreamt of a summer moon and arching trees, or of fairy boats a-sail upon it; just where the moonshine flickered at one side of the garden, Martin could have fancied that the parterre was dreaming of summer, its treasures, of blushing roses and stately lilies. He looked for Ella's window, it was hidden in shadow, the wind swept by with a moaning gust, and it rustled the dead leaves at his feet, while the house-dog set up a long, deep bay; his footsteps had aroused it.

"Oh, Ella; oh, my wife, for whom I would die, to whom I am nothing—you are sleeping and forgetting me, or remembering me only with a smile of half-amused pity. Oh! my life is full to the brim of bitterness; will *she* ever awaken? Shall I ever win fame and fortune? shall I ever return and say, come to me, my wife! come, and share my life? or shall I sink down and die, after striving in vain? shall I die, and release her from her rash oath? Never, oh, stars of the night; never, scornful, sailing moon; never, black, thunderous clouds; never, sobbing, rushing wind; never, mysterious womb of nature, in which all things lie hidden until the uprising of the spring shall call their beauties into life, and clothe the world again in living green; never, earth and sky, and elements, and heart of man; never, Ella, Ella Thorpe! think not the starving cur will forego his prey; I will strive and strive, I will work with my brains, I will work with my hands; I will grind down my life, I will forego my youth, I will toil for wealth, and then—then, if I fail—hear me, dreaming woods, and listening winds, and wild night, hear me swear that I will return and claim Ella; though I be clothed in tatters, though my arm be branded with a felon's mark, and though she be the queen of the lordliest drawing-room in all Europe, she shall follow me, shall come to my arms, she shall lie at my heart, she shall be my wife!" and the schoolmaster looked once more towards that window which was Ella's, but which the shadows hid from him, and then he left Alton Hall, and it was long before he saw again *the face* of his wife.

CHAPTER XI.

LIFE OR DEATH.

WAS Macnellan to live or to die? This question sat at the door of his room, sounded in the footsteps of the attendants, was printed upon the anxious face of his physician, was debated eagerly in the family councils of the Thorpes; daily the bland mesmeriser glided up the stairs, waved his white hands over the face of the sufferer, and left him in a sound, deep sleep. "The glass of Time," with its minute hand oscillating between the two great words "Life and Death," was eagerly consulted; the man was hardly alive, still less was he dead. With his brain in that state he was, of course, powerless to damage his hosts, his lawyers could not act for him under the circumstances, and it seemed he had not a friend to inquire after his well being; he had not a relation in the world, and he had been too bitter and caustic a cynic to have allowed any of those parasites around him who usually follow in the train of the rich.

"I want an heir," he said to Doctor Molson, one day. "I have not a creature in the world. I have a great mind to bequeath all my money to St. Jude's Hospital."

The St. Jude's Hospital was dear unto the heart of good, honourable Doctor Molson, but he said that he could listen to nothing of the kind while his patient's brain was still so excited.

It was one day about the middle of January, a dark day, fog lay low over the country, the air was raw, it was a day to turn from the window with a shudder and to come and consult the face of the fire as the face of a friend.

Thorpe stood in his rich library with his eyes upon the blazing coals, which burned brilliantly in the low grate. Mrs. Thorpe was knitting, her usual employment, upon the low, soft, luxurious sofa.

"What time do we dine to-day?" asked Thorpe, at last.

"At five o'clock."

"Humph! this kind of suspense will drive me mad; I would rather, far rather, he claimed the amount of his note of hand, and we could leave. I should speculate in the New Canal Company, there is a fortune to be realized *there*! it would take three years' income from your settlement, and we should be richer than Macnellan in twelve months."

"You have had enough of speculating, Francis."

"No, I have not. I have had just enough to lose, that's all. Macnellan, you know made the bulk of *his* property by speculations."

"He is more lucky than you are."

"Well," said Thorpe, with a slight laugh, "I think *he is* lucky. What other man could have been run down and smashed by an engine, and yet appear as much like living as he does? By George, I think he will recover."

"It will be serious for us if he does," said Mrs. Thorpe; "he seems to be forgetting Ella, too, now. I think if he recovers he will be such a wreck of himself, that all those kind of feelings will be dead in him. I should not wonder if he did not take a great hatred to her, and all his thoughts will be concentrated on vengeance, and money making; not only will he claim his eighty thousand, but he will injure your character in the mercantile world, and bring other creditors around you."

"Of course he will. And a man of his wealth there is no standing against; if I brought a charge of defamation against him, the few thousands the court might award me would be a drop in the bucket of my liabilities, just like putting a thimblefull of water before a thirsty ox. And then how are we to live in the meanwhile? I must go to Emms, and take to gambling, I suppose," and he laughed bitterly.

"It is really most serious. Let us just take a fair estimate of our liabilities and possessions, and see how we stand; shall we?"

"If *you* like; I have gone through it all until I am quite sick of the affair. This house and grounds are worth twenty thousand pounds, and we have eighty thousand in the funds; we have eight hundred a year by our marriage settlement, and we have furniture, horses, carriages, pictures and jewels to the amount of another sixty thousand.

"Well!"

"We have, then, one hundred and sixty thousand pounds."

"Well!"

"We only owe Macnellan eighty thousand."

"Then you forget the forty thousand pounds worth of dividends to the Mining Company?"

"They would wait."

"Ah! yes; if it were not for Macnellan, we might retrench and pay off a great deal of that by instalments."

"Then we have eighty thousand left?"

"Yes; but remember by that time house, grounds, horses, furniture, jewels, pictures, will be gone."

Mrs. Thorpe looked wretched. Her passion (if she had a passion) was for diamonds and Dresden, and rich furniture; she had heaped these things around her, and now some of them, at least, must go to the hammer.

"Well," said Thorpe, after a pause, "properly invested, that eighty thousand will bring in more than three thousand a year; your income will make nearly four thousand."

"It is not so very bad then," said Mrs. Thorpe.

"That depends upon what you call bad. Our income here is no longer a reality now that the mines have failed, but we must take into consideration two or three thousand pounds worth of private debts. We shall, in fact, if we sell everything but our clothes, be reduced to three thousand a year."

"And actually," said Mrs. Thorpe, smiling sadly, "you told poor Ella that if she did not marry Macnellan we should have only my income!"

"Well," said Thorpe, rather loudly, "of course I did not take your gewgaws into consideration."

"The gewgaws," said Mrs. Thorpe, "will become useful after all."

"It's a confoundedly cursed mess to get into!" said Thorpe, sitting down. "We shall have to take a house in one of the squares, furnish it, set up a Brougham, and give tea parties. Ugh! how poor, how shabbily genteel we shall become; and Ella on hand, and Arthur to send to Oxford!"

"Oh, we had much better go abroad," said Mrs. Thorpe.

"I detest life abroad," answered Thorpe.

"If Macnellan would only die without making a will, there is only the note of hand to prove the debt."

"Where is it?" whispered Mrs. Thorpe.

"In London, safely lodged with his lawyer," said Thorpe, bitterly.

"But if he were dead?"

"Oh, yes; if he were dead," said Thorpe, "it would be all right, he has no heir at all."

Mrs. Thorpe sighed, and put down her knitting. "One can't help wishing him dead," she said.

"One can't help wishing to help him on the way," said Thorpe, poking the fire. "And if," he added, speaking low, and motioning towards his wife, "if I could ship him off to Canaan's shore without suspicion—*I'd do it.*"

Mrs. Thorpe grew white.

"Don't talk in that manner, Francis," she said.

"Humbug! You know you have thought the same thing over and over to yourself, only it shocks you to hear another voice utter the words. If you had a mad, dangerous, suffering dog, would you not have him shot? This man is more dangerous to us than any mad dog, and his loss will be felt by no living creature. If reason progresses as it seems to be doing, people will look at these things in a very different manner in another century. Even now, it is no uncommon thing to hear educated people, in good society, cordially and openly express their wish for the death of any one particular bad or useless person. People will soon proceed from talking to doing."

"Francis!"

"Hold your tongue; let me talk," said Thorpe, in a rapid, fretful whisper, beginning to pace up and down on the hearth-rug. "Say the Government wants to make war, does it scruple to sacrifice forty lives—forty thousand lives to its interest? Look how our people shattered the Sepoys to atoms at the cannon's mouth the other day in India—even some that had been innocent, they say—and do you dare to tell me that I am worse than other men in wishing to remove my enemy? Place anybody else in my position, and see how he would act. Place Macnellan himself—ha! ha! ha!—he'd not have waited so long. Don't talk trash to me!"

Mrs. Thorpe only uttered one word, but it was eloquent with meaning.

"Detection," she said.

"There you have me!" Thorpe came to a stand-still upon the rug. "There you have me; that's all I dread, not the crime itself, it would not trouble my conscience in the least. I could get a mortgage on this place at once; then to pay off the dividends, or half of them, and we could go on here swimmingly. I should have a try at this Canal Company, and all would be right again."

"It is not the least use to talk," said Mrs. Thorpe, "you know you could not do such a thing without detection."

"Do you mean to tell me that half the

people one meets at balls and dinner parties have not done the same thing? There are more undiscovered *murders*, if one must use the word, than discovered ones. It's all a matter of being found out, confound it; *I wish I could poison him cleverly.*" The words went up to Heaven's high Tabernacle, as Sterne would say, the outspoken words of a man who had conceived murder in his heart; his eyes looked so very sinister, that the wife involuntarily shuddered. "Now look here, would you help me in this?"

"Oh, Francis, I could not! I could not!"

"Is it conscience, or dread of detection?"

"Both, both!"

"Well, then, let him recover, and let everything go to wreck."

"We shall have clear consciences, we shall have three thousand a-year, we shall do very well."

"We shall have bread and milk, and morning prayers, and Kidderminster carpets in the drawing-room," said Thorpe, in a mocking whisper. "If I were you, Maria, I would set up a Dorcas meeting and turn Methodist."

"Macnellan may die, after all," said Mrs. Thorpe.

"But the anxiety will kill me before then, he may linger for a year. Oh, if I had only a clever secret! I have sat up late in the library studying poisons."

"Francis!"

"Well, confound you, why do you hiss my name out like that. If you would help me, I could lay that rascal safely in his winding sheet before the week was over."

"For God's sake, don't!" said the wife with energy. "You will be discovered. Molson is keen, and shrewd, and clever."

"But unsuspicious, utterly unsuspicious."

Just then a light step in the hall, the door opened, and Ella came into the room; she had been crying.

"What is the matter, Ella?"

"Oh, nothing, mamma, only it's so dull, so very dreadfully dull here."

"Poor thing," said Thorpe, "I don't see the least why she shouldn't go and visit the Kilrudereys; they have asked her."

"Oh, yes, do, do let me go," said Ella, vehemently. "I do so long to go to London. Alton is hateful at this time of the year, with no visitors. I am sure you and Kate Hall are enough to take care of poor Mac, he hardly ever thinks about me now."

"Then I will write," said Mrs. Thorpe, "and accept the Kilrudereys' invitation. You can go on Monday, and take Fanny with you."

"Oh, thank you, thank you," she began to jump about the room joyfully.

"Ella, I suppose the idea of marrying Macnellan is as repugnant to you as ever," asked her step-father.

"Worse, ten thousand times worse!" she spoke quite passionately.

"I could have fancied from your violence, child, that you were in love with somebody else," said Thorpe, who was striving to reassure his wife and quiet his own nerves, by talking of what he thought trifles.

"Challoner," said Mrs. Thorpe, smiling, and falling into her husband's vein ; she felt it refreshing to talk innocently again. "Challoner was poor Ella's fancy."

"A dressed up nincompoop," said Thorpe, in a tone of contempt.

"That he was," said Ella, warmly. They laughed and chatted, so it was settled that Ella was to go to London.

CHAPTER XII.

A SMALL LOAN.

The days rolled on; Monday came, Ella and Fanny and their portmanteaux, went off in the travelling carriage to St. Jude's, and it returned empty in the afternoon; the house felt very desolate. Kate Hall was always busy with her needle, there was so much to be done now in trimming and re-trimming Ella's dresses, and in sending them after her to the gay Kilrudereys, who were as full of parties and balls in their villa at Sydenham as it was possible to be. At Alton all was dull. Kate Hall looked very ill; is it any use to hide that for Martin Cruize she had entertained a lively admiration? and his unfortunate speech about the "Hill-side" had made her imagine that he returned it; from that time, what had been liking had ripened into a disinterested, warm affection; his disgraceful and sudden dismissal had pained her much; then the way in which Ella had excited herself about it astonished her. She had thought her heartless, but now she came back to her first idea of her, that she was kind. She hardly knew if the schoolmaster *was* in love with Ella; she hoped not, and tried to believe not. She had been too timid to seek him for a parting interview, and now "his place in her poor life seemed vacant," for she did not pine, she only blamed herself for having misconstrued his words and looks. She went on sewing her life away; how often she felt it "dreadfully dull" did not matter; she was born to a cheerless, dull grey life, like thousands of others; she had not a very restless spirit, although there were times when it would joyfully have plumed its wings and flown away to other scenes. She was sewing as usual in the small parlour, when she saw a young man pass the window by the shrubbery; there was thick snow on the ground, and the young man's iron shoes made deep marks in it. She rushed at once to the window and tapped at it, the young man looked up; he was a tall, rather handsome fellow, dressed in a kind of half groom half gentleman fashion; he came to the window when she tapped it; it was a French one, and she opened it.

"Stop a moment, George," she said, "let me bring you a mat to wipe your feet upon."

She brought him one, and the young man wiped his feet, and then stooped and kissed Kate Hall.

"You didn't expect to see me, my girl," he said, in rather a countrified accent.

"No, George, I thought you were in Liverpool, you were last week."

"I couldn't stand it any longer, my girl,"

said George, sitting down near the fire and closing his eyes sleepily.

George was a little drunk, George was nearly always a little drunk. He was Kate's only brother, who had preyed upon her scanty earnings all her life, and who was perpetually losing his situations. He was not qualified to write for a lawyer, on account of his loose habits. This was the cause of Kate's grey gingham dresses, and sober cheap clothing; George never left her an extra shilling to bless herself with.

"I want you to help me with a small loan, my girl," said George, pathetically, "I've hardly a rag to my back."

"How much?" faltered Kate.

"Five pounds will do," said George, half asleep by this time.

Poor Kate sighed but she could not refuse, she had but four pounds ten in the world. George had been draining her purse lately, and her quarter would not be due again until March.

"I haven't five pounds, George," she said.

"Well, let us see what you have?"

"I will give you three pounds," so she went upstairs, and when she came down again George was standing by the window. She put the three sovereigns into his hand: "George, dear, I wish you would try and keep your situations longer."

"I'm not going to bother my head about situations any more, my girl."

"What are you going to do?"

"Never mind," said George, closing one eye and looking knowing, "I have a very good friend, who has put me up to a thing or two."

"I hope, dear George, that you are careful what friends you make. You are too confiding."

"I'm all right," said George. "I say, have you the key of that sideboard? can you give me a drop of brandy?"

"No; at least, I should not like to."

"Do they keep you strict?"

"No, I don't mean that, but brandy is very bad for you, George," and tears of sorrow and regret for the wasted life, which owed its spring to the same source as her own, gathered thickly in her eyes, and rained upon his hands, which she was holding.

George drew his away.

"Don't blubber, my girl," he said, but not unkindly, "don't make a fuss because I asked for a drop of brandy. I'm as cold as death."

"I will get you a cup of hot coffee made in the French fashion in an instant, and a nice little loaf, and some cold meat."

George had not breakfasted yet.

"I think I could eat some," said he.

"Oh! George, it is a home you want, and somebody to look after your comforts. You would never drink then, if we could only afford to live together."

"I must have a nice little wife, I suppose," said George. "I wish I could get one with two or three hundred pounds."

"I wish you could get one to love you, and-look after your comforts, and keep you steady, dear."

Then Kate went to the housekeeper and asked for some breakfast for her brother. She was a prodigous favourite in the kitchen, two or three servants began to busy themselves about her brother's breakfast; they pitied him for his walk in the cold, they put cream into the coffee, and cut the nicest slices off the roast beef.

She took him in the tray herself, and pressed him to eat a good breakfast. He began with something like appetite, but after the first two or three mouthsful he put down his knife and fork, and declared he could not eat any more.

"You are not well, George. Do take some coffee, dear."

He drank the coffee, and seemed to like it.

"George, have you walked far this morning?"

"Yes, from Dogly Wood, and I slept at the inn there last night."

"Why, that's five miles from here."

"Nearer six."

"And yet you have no appetite. George, you can't be well!"

"I'm all right, my girl."

"Where are you going to from here?"

"To London, my girl, that's the only place for a man to get on in."

Kate sighed heavily, and thought of somebody who was trying to work his way on in London, and who was perhaps as badly off as her brother, and without a sister to help him.

"And now, my girl," said George, "I'll go—thank you for your small loan. I shall start by third-class train to London to-night, from St. Jude's."

"And your friend is there, dear?"

"Yes."

"Do tell me what he is."

"He is in a very large way of business," said George.

"What business?"

"A general merchant," said George, shortly.

Poor Kate saw that George was not inclined to let her into his plans: she sighed sorrowfully.

"Kate, you are enough to drive a man wild, to look at your long face. I hope if I do get a wife, she'll be a cheerful one."

Kate's feelings were so much wounded by this cruel speech that she burst into tears.

"What's the matter now? what's the girl fooling about?" said the brother.

Just then Mrs. Thorpe came into the room. Kate hastened to explain it was her brother, whom she had not seen for a year; he had walked over from Dogly Wood; she had taken the liberty to provide him with breakfast.

Mrs. Thorpe gave George, who stood up blushing and looking foolish, a cold stare, in a careless manner; just then she had other things to think of than Catherine, her brother, or his breakfast.

"Oh, yes," she said, "quite right."

And she went out again, and left the Halls together.

"She is rather a fine woman," said George, who pretended to be a great connoisseur in women's beauty.

"Do you think so?" said Kate.

"She's a fine figure and fine eyes," said George.

"You ought to see Miss Thorpe," said Kate.

"Where is she?" said George, with *empressement.*

"In London now."

"Ah, bother, what's the use of telling a fellow of a fine girl a hundred and odd miles away from him? Well, indeed, my girl, I must go."

And again George kissed her, and after a few more parting words Kate was left alone. She went to her room, knelt down by her bedside, and wept. She prayed afterwards, then arose, and bathed her eyes, and returned to the little sitting-room and her sewing.

CHAPTER XIII.

PAULINE'S IMPATIENCE.

WHILE January snow lay deep, while winds howled, and winter gaieties went on in town and country, the Leslies were sinking deeper and deeper into debt and poverty at "Crane's Farm." Somehow or other, Mr. Leslie always contrived to keep the larder well supplied; he got credit, or came mysteriously into the possession of small sums, varying from five shillings to five pounds; but his rent remained unpaid, his St. Jude's creditors pestered him, he had one or two threats of summonses to the County Court, but he bore all with tolerable equanimity. Towards his wife and boys he was always brutal, to Pauline subservient and lover-like. It was a mysterious link, that between this girl and himself. Conjectures, wild as detrimental to the young lady, were formed by the country gossips. The Yardlys were completely puzzled, and unable to solve the mystery. The wife and daughters of the Vicar were quite above calling on unknown parishioners, reported poor; but the Vicar himself did occasionally condescend to pay them a visit. He always found the wife sad and silent, Leslie smiling and bland, Pauline lady-like and lively. Towards her too, Leslie was a devoted inamorato. It was passing strange, it was marvellous. Was she his daughter, and not Mrs. Leslie's? Was she neither of their daughters? was she Leslie's mistress? but no, impossible, the great difference in their ages and his poverty forbade such an idea. Then what was she? The neighbourhood refused to accept her as she represented herself—as Leslie's step-daughter — that is, they did not openly refuse, but few believed it in their hearts.

One January morning, when the boys were playing in the snow, when Mrs. Leslie was mending old clothes, and Leslie was smoking in the arm-chair, Pauline came into the room, wrapped in a short, loose dressing-gown, her hair in papers; she looked the impersonation of untidy deshabille; her face was unwashed, there was a cloud upon her brow of extreme discontent. She sat on the ground before the fire, and held her hands towards the flame.

"Pauline, how untidy you look," said Mrs. Leslie, looking up from her work; "your face is not washed, and your hair in papers, it's disgraceful."

"Hold your bother," said Pauline.

"There is one thing certain," said Leslie, "that if my pet lamb never washed her face at all, it would still be the most lovely face in England."

"What's the good of beauty, or anything else here, in this hole," said Pauline, "horrible, dreadful place, I wish I was dead."

"My darling!"

"Oh, papa, I am sorry to annoy you. I know you can't help it; but if ever a poor wretch was tired of her life, I am that one!"

"You have not the least patience, angel; wait just a little while, and I will take you to Paris, and you shall go to balls every night."

"James, what nonsense you talk," said the wife.

"Thank you, perhaps I do, but I must say I cannot compliment you on the superior brilliancy of *your* conversation; I never hear anything but fault-finding fall from your lips."

"I cannot imagine why you don't charge this Mr. Thorpe for the mesmerising."

"Perhaps you would like me to go and set up in that line?"

"I should like you to go and set up in any

honest line, whereby you might earn your bread and keep out of debt."

"Pauline, just listen to her, is it not edifying, is it not a privilege to have such an excellent woman in the house, always ready with an extemporaneous sermon on morality?"

"Her preaching drives me mad," cried Pauline, "I wish something would happen. Nothing will ever happen in this horrid place; fancy, we shall have been twelve months here in April."

"Shall have been, dearest—we shan't be here then, we shall be in Paris, Vienna, Rome, wherever you like."

"Such a horrible life as we have had here, papa. How could you, how can you stand it, you that have been used to such gay doings, to such life?"

"*Je suis perdu ici en peu,*" said Leslie, for the little servant came in with the table cloth and knives. Leslie meant that he was hiding from his numerous creditors in London and elsewhere. But now dinner was the great event to be considered, and he began to lecture Lizzie about the basting of the fowl, and the frizzling of the sausages. When she was gone, Leslie took up the change she had put down out of a shilling, there was a battered fourpenny bit of the reign of George II.

"That's a treasure," said Pauline, "one does not often get money of that date."

"If it is a treasure," said Mrs. Leslie, significantly, "I hope you will take care of it."

"Not if it be wanted for the use of the house," said Pauline; "here, papa;" he took it and kissed the tips of her fingers.

"Oh! *I wish, I wish* I knew what your grand scheme was, papa," said Pauline, "I believe it will end in nothing like all the rest."

"Why, you most unjust pussy, when did ever papa promise you more than he performed? but now I promise you more than ever, I promise you a fortune."

"God knows where it is to come from!" groaned Mrs. Leslie.

"Just so," said Leslie, turning towards her, "he does know, he is supposed to know everything, therefore it may be conjectured that he knows that."

"Blasphemy," said Mrs. Leslie.

"Not at all; you make an assertion, and I echo it."

"Yours is a mocking tongue, James Leslie, and you have a hard heart, a cruel heart."

"I wish I had a hard bag of gold," said Leslie, "then you might preach or talk till 'kingdom come' if you liked."

"I wish we were out of this place," said Pauline.

"I wish we were out of debt," said Mrs. Leslie, sternly.

"Confound you, why don't you go?" said Leslie, "why do you stay here living upon credit, if it pricks your conscience so much? Nobody wants you here."

"My children, James, are the only ties that bind me to you, the boys would be murdered without me."

Pauline burst out into loud derisive laughter.

"Why, papa, anybody would think you were a felon in disguise."

Leslie hardly smiled at this, but turning impatiently towards the fire, he said—

"What a liar and fool that woman is."

That woman did not answer.

Soon after the dinner came in, Pauline sat down to it in the curling papers and dressing gown. Mrs. Leslie did not dare to call the poor boys in until the meal was over; then she went out to them and brought in the poor things, rosy with cold, and hungry as wolves. They sat down timidly to the odds and ends of the fowls, and some tepid potatoes; they each got a severe ear boxing while they sat at meat, for some real or supposed fault. After dinner Arnold was called by Pauline to repeat his alphabet; he had quite forgotten A,

B and C, so he stood stammering, and she struck him with the book.

"You don't hit half-hard enough, Pauline," said Leslie, "not half;" so the fair Pauline tried her best to improve in that line, and succeeded so well that Arnold set up a shout of pain; then Mrs. Leslie hurried both her boys into the farm kitchen, and Leslie and Pauline were left alone. The untidy beauty went and sat on a low stool at Leslie's feet, and leaned the back of her fair dishevelled tresses against his arm.

"Do tell me your plan, papalie."

"No, dearest, could not possibly, it would spoil all."

"Has it anything to do with those Thorpes?"

"Perhaps so, and perhaps not."

"Ah, papa, it must be something about the rich, sick old man, eh?"

Leslie only smiled.

"Perhaps so, and perhaps not."

"Ah! papa, I wish he'd die, take a fancy to you, and leave you all his money."

"I wish he would, but he must take a fancy to me before he dies."

"And has he not?"

Leslie bethought him of the very evident dislike and distrust which the patient always manifested for him, but he answered as before—

"Perhaps so, and perhaps not."

"Provoking papalie,"—so she could get nothing from him. Soon after Mrs. Leslie came in, and sat down to what Pauline called her eternal sewing.

CHAPTER XIV.

A NIGHT AT ALTON HALL.

It was one windy night in the village of Alton, the snow was drifted about in heaps, the cold was piercing; the moon only showed her face at intervals, the sky was black. It was a night when timid children cried in their beds; the wind went about making such weird sounds, it shrieked like a Banshee about the walls and verandahs of Alton Hall.

Thorpe and his wife were in bed and asleep, the three men servants were also buried in that deep refreshing rest which manual labour brings as its own reward; the six maid servants were all asleep. Macnellan was also buried in repose. Leslie had been with him in the evening, and had succeeded in casting him into a profound slumber, and by his side the old hired nurse nodded in her cushioned chair.

Kate Hall had that night accepted the post of extra watcher, so as to relieve the servants, and of all the household she was the only one who was wakeful. She sat by the fire, and heaped more coals on, for the night was bitter. Thought, and memory, and anxiety kept her wakeful; she felt, too, an oppression at the chest and a pain in the side, which might have caused her alarm had she been of a nervous temperament. She looked up once at the ormulu clock over the chimney piece, the hands pointed to twelve, and then she arranged her ideas. Again she began to think of Martin, his kind voice, his pleasant smile, his admiring eyes, for they had been admiring when looking at Kate and when Ella was not by—did he love her? She went over the problem again and again, and still a dull voice in her heart of hearts answered—no! Then she thought of Ella; did he love her? Then she checked herself and thought of the patient on the bed, of the mysteries of life and death, of the awfulness of eternity, of her own state; she thought of the last with calm hope, her life below had been so sad that she had perforce raised her eyes to the untasted joys above.

Poor Kate! the clock ticked, the old nurse snored, the coals fell noisily into the grate, as coals do at night when people are watching alone; tick, tick went the clock, the nurse now snored terrifically. Kate began to pace the room, the wind howled and shrieked hideously about the roof. Presently Kate heard a scratching sound under the window, as though somebody was filing or sharpening some tool. She listened, and forgot it again; presently she heard a distinct sound out on the balcony like the tramping of feet, but it subsided again.

She murmured to herself that the wind made strange noises on wild nights like that one, and she raised her heart in prayer that no accident might occur from falling roof or chimney stacks, then she went again to the fire. She heard nothing for ten minutes, it was now half-past one; she snuffed the candles, for their wicks had grown so large that the room was darkened, and the curtains and wardrobe began to take fantastic shapes; but with the snuffing of the candles and poking of the fire came increased sense of security. But immediately there sounded through the house a wild agonised yell; it broke upon the other and lesser noises of the night with an indescribable horror. Catherine's heart beat fast, but the nurse slumbered on, as did Macnellan. Was it only the chimera of an excited brain? or had that shriek really disturbed the watches of the night? The next instant all was still as death, but even while Kate listened, another noise came to her ears, the sound of many feet were on the stairs. Impelled by a cowardly instinct she was rushing to secure the door, but reflecting that perhaps somebody below might stand in need of help she caught up the poker, poor, brave gentle terrified Kate, and forced back the door. Upon the stairs stood a crowd of rough, ragged, brutal men, armed with bludgeons, and one or two with pistols. Kate's head swam and she nearly fell, but she would not faint.

"What do you want?" she gasped.

A brute who stood near raised the butt end of a pistol, and would have struck her down, but one of his companions drew back his arm.

"What do you want?" repeated Kate, whose courage seemed to rise suddenly with the emergency, and who seemed strangely carried out of herself at this moment.

"We wan't all the money the old sick beggar has about him; that's his room, go in and wake him, or I'll knock your brains out and his."

Every face was blackened, so that Kate could not distinguish one of the thieves from another.

"Where are the servants?" was her first cry.

The next moment she reflected that three would have poor chance against six or seven; there was nothing for it but to waken Macnellan. She bent over him and touched his face, he awoke with a muttered oath, and there round his bed stood a crowd of ruffians with blackened faces, dressed in rags of the worst description.

"Devils!" he cried "devils! come from hell—ha! ha! ha!"

"No," said Kate, "robbers, who threaten to murder us all."

"If you don't give up what money you have about you, I smash your brains about the sheets!"

"I—?" Macnellan stared wildly. "I've only a hundred pounds in my dressing-case."

"That will do," from the ruffian who seemed to be the spokesman; all the rest guarded a profound silence.

"Hand it over; quick, old codger, or we'll spread your brains over the bed clothes."

Kate brought his dressing-case, the robber broke it open and counted over the money he found there; it was rather more than a hundred pounds in gold. This he pocketed, and then said to Kate—

"Come down and hand us the plate, it's no use to scream, we've tied all the men servants' legs, and quieted every body in the house; take us down to the plate, or we'll quiet you!"

All through this the old nurse snored and slumbered, and Kate, as though in a dream, led the way down to the housekeeper's room where the plate chest was fixed into the wall.

"I have not the key," said she.

"You know where 'tis."

She knew it was on the bunch of keys in Mrs. Thorpe's dressing-room.

"I will go and fetch it," she said.

The spokesman twisted her arm brutally, but she never winced.

"You shall take me upstairs to find it."

Horror chained Kate to the spot, she dreaded to find herself alone with that ruffian.

"I can't," she said, "unless somebody else will come. I am afraid of you."

There was a muttered whisper, and then another man came up.

"Be quick," said he, "quick, if you value your life."

She went then hastily up the stairs towards Mrs. Thorpe's room. She found the door ajar; she went in, the night lamp was flickering faintly, and on the floor lay Mrs. Thorpe in her night dress, bleeding profusely from a wound in the temple. Kate coupled that with the yell, and yet she never shrieked nor fell; she went forward to where the keys hung.

"Take them," she said, and she flung them to the man.

"Find them," said the man, and Kate knelt,

and by the flickering light singled out the key and gave it to the man; he rushed off with it. Then she bent down and found that Mrs. Thorpe still breathed; she bathed her wound and put her in the bed; the poor lady moaned terribly, but did not recover her consciousness. Then Kate went into the next room where Mr. Thorpe slept; he gave a shriek, cowardly as that of a woman, when he saw the light, but on recognising Kate, he exclaimed:

"What have they done? Is any body murdered? How did they get in?"

"I don't know," said Kate. "Get up, Mr. Thorpe, and come with me to call the men servants."

"I can't, they have tied me to the bed!" and so they had, with strong cords evidently brought for the purpose.

It took so long to hunt up a pair of scissors, and then to work with their blunt edges through the ropes, that by the time Mr. Thorpe stood upon his feet Kate felt sure the burglars had escaped with their booty. Mr. Thorpe thrust on some clothes, and then stood undecided in the room.

"If they are about the passages," he said tremulously, "they will murder us as sure as fate—there are a dozen of them!"

"Half a dozen or so."

"Where are they now?"

"Ransacking the plate chest."

"The servants must be in league with them," said Mr. Thorpe. "I never heard them break in. I knew nothing until I heard Mrs. Thorpe scream. Have they hurt her?"

"They have cut her head open!" said Kate, hoping to rouse him from his cowardly apathy.

"I rushed towards her room, and they forced me back to the bed and tied me down."

"Hark!"

They heard steps again on the stairs, the next moment two half-dressed maid servants rushed into the room. One, who had not been so well secured as the rest, had managed to get at her penknife, which was hanging in the pocket of her dress over the bed, and she had liberated her bedfellow, and afterwards the other women, some of whom had gone in to see about the men servants.

"Let us all go down in a body," said Kate, valorously, "let us go and call the men," and she actually led the way towards the men servants' apartment, but on the way they met all the servants in a heap, the women now sobbing and screaming in hysterics, the men with frightened faces. Mostyn, a new footman from London, looked particularly white and horror stricken; the other two, who had lived some time in the family, seemed enraged and clamorous for vengeance on the miscreants, who had, they declared, surprised them in their deep sleep, and stood over them with pistols, and clubs, and threats. Mostyn looked most uncomfortable, and on him Mr. Thorpe cast a suspicious glance.

"Where are they now?" said Kate Hall.

Alas, the men had got down too late, the plate chest had been nearly emptied, and the robbers were gone.

"They cannot have been gone long," said Kate, "rouse the villagers in pursuit at once!"

"Useless in the darkness of the night, and at this hour," said Thorpe. "In the morning we must send into St. Jude for the constables, and write and put the police and a London detective on the scent."

"I would have them followed now," said Kate, but nobody stirred.

And then the question was mooted, how had they broken in? So now that the plate was lost, and the robbers gone, the whole party went down in a body to reconnoitre and ascertain the extent of loss and damage. Spoons, forks, cream jugs, tea and coffee services, silver cover dishes, &c., were gone. All the doors were securely locked; then they went round to the front. Nobody had broken in there. Afterwards they went into the dining-room under Macnellan's chamber, and there the whole side of the window had been cleverly filed out; the robbers had climbed upon the low balcony, filed out the glass, and then sawn through the shutter. Of course none but a gang of regular burglars, well provided with proper instruments, could have effected this, and the extreme noise of the wind had conspired to drown the noises they made. Afterwards they had mounted to the servants' rooms, and bound and quieted them; they had stuffed the bedclothes into the womens' mouths to stop their screaming. The men servants now formed a blockade of tables and presses against the open window, and Kate called out, "Mrs. Thorpe, she may be dying! Run for a doctor!"

So long before daylight, some of the villagers were aroused, and sent into St. Jude's for Doctor Molson. Kate went upstairs again to Mrs. Thorpe, and bathed her temples with brandy, and presently the poor lady spoke.

"Have I been ill?" said she, "do tell me what has happened."

So Kate told her as gently as she could.

She gave an agonised shriek, almost as terrible as the one she had uttered before she was struck down. "My diamonds, my diamonds," she said, "I was trying to save them, they are worth thirty thousand pounds; look, look, quick, is my jewel-box gone?"

Kate went to the dressing table. Alas; the pretty dressing case, with its treasures of rubies, and golden bracelets, and its wealth of diamonds was gone. Mrs. Thorpe was more moved than we have ever seen her; the cut in her head was nothing to the loss of the diamonds.

"My beautiful set bought in Paris. I saw a villain with my box, that was the first thing I saw. I was awakened by his stumbling against the table; he was a stout man. Oh! if I could find him; and I sprang out of bed when I saw him with my jewel-box. I screamed, and he cut me down with his club."

Kate tried to soothe her, and told her of the Detective who was to be sent for; she represented to her that the large and heavy booty the thieves had carried off must lead of itself to their detection. Afterwards she crept down stairs to try in her quiet way to set things to rights. In the passage near the house-keeper's closet, her foot tripped against something; she took it up, it was a pocket book, shabby, and horrible to relate, blood-stained. Probably one of the thieves had cut his hand with the glass of the window. She opened the book, surely this would lead to something. Kate took it to the window, and the name she read there sent a thrill of sickening terror through her frame. She had but one thought—to destroy this witness of the crime of one, only too dear to her, and Kate went into the kitchen where the fire was now burning, and unobserved, she watched the tell-tale pocket-book consume away; then she went to her room, and to bed, for she was very ill, and Doctor Molson had three patients to attend to when he arrived at Alton Hall.

CHAPTER XV.

"DIAMONDS ARE AS GOOD AS SOVEREIGNS."

Of course the whole country rang with the account of the daring and dreadful burglary. Detectives were put upon the scent, and three of the burglars were discovered in a den in London. Some of the plate was traced and recovered; some of it was smelted down, and irrevocably lost, and three of the ruffians were brought to trial; they refused to name their accomplices, and to say if they knew anything of Mrs. Thorpe's diamonds, which were *never recovered.* Diamonds are as good as sovereigns; whoever had obtained those jewels was enriched, but it was in vain that all the pawnbrokers and receiving houses were searched. Mrs. Thorpe never saw her beloved ornaments again. The men, who were each sentenced to ten years' penal servitude, were well known to the police; it seems they formed part of a desperate gang, the chief of which was supposed to have bagged the diamonds; this man had never shewn himself in London, or elsewhere since the robbery, and it was surmised, that he had escaped to the Continent, but all search for him proved vain. Among the names of the condemned men the *one which Kate had found in the pocket-book* did not appear. She, poor thing, drooped from that day, and Doctor Molson gave it as his opinion that consumption had set in.

Where was she to go to be nursed, poor, friendless one? Was not one patient enough for the Thorpes'; could they be expected to nurse her? They could not have her in the house, but they sent her down to the lodge-keeper's cottage, and they were on the whole kind to her. It was a dreadful loss to the Thorpes'—that of the diamonds.

"Diamonds are as good as sovereigns," as Mrs. Thorpe said. "It is the same as though I had lost thirty thousand pounds."

Macnellan was slowly recovering, his lucid intervals were more frequent, his fever subsided, his wounds healed. Thorpe did not hold another such conversation with his wife again for weeks after the burglary. She was too ill and weak to assist him with his counsels, and Thorpe was too cowardly to act without them.

Ella did not return; she wrote to offer to come and nurse her mother, but Mrs. Thorpe felt glad to be rid of her exuberent life and spirits for a time, so she wrote to put her off, and Ella—unlike many affectionate daughters, who would have flown to their sick mother, even in utter disregard of their commands—Ella consented to remain in London.

Mr. Leslie still called every day to mesmerise Macnellan.

For a long time after the burglary, deep into the wet weeks of February, and almost to the borders of the dry, bright cold days of naked, boisterous March, policemen walked mysteriously about the grounds and house of Alton; the recovered part of the booty was again locked up in the plate chest. Great excitement prevailed as the time of the trial drew near. Macnellan himself took an interest in dwelling upon the circumstances of the robbery; he was less outwardly insulting now, but the few things he did say made Thorpe tremble; he found that the revenge of the maimed and crippled man would be complete, he meant to exact payment to the last farthing. Thirty thousand pounds' worth of their property was gone. Alton Hall must be sold, there was not a doubt on the subject, and there would be actually only Mrs. Thorpe's settlement, and the produce of the sale of the pictures to depend upon, for Macnellan meant to urge the mining company to press for the forty thousand pounds' worth of dividends; he intended to let their creditors know that Thorpe was not a rich man; he told him so, quietly enough, one day, and Thorpe felt mad with impotent rage and terror. Genteel poverty, that which his pride so much hated, was before him. Macnellan's rage and spite towards Ella knew no bounds, he held his tongue about her now that his brain fever was over, but Mrs. Thorpe could read real hatred in his cold eye whenever the girl's name was mentioned, his illness and excessive sufferings, had completely cured him of his infatuated, and sensual passion, but they had left another one more terrible, perhaps more dangerous; he *hated her*, and when Macnellan hated he usually crushed.

* * * *

The trial was over, the three burglars were sentenced to their ten long years of punishment. The March winds had blown themselves away, and were howling wildly enough over the Atlantic Ocean, but soft, rich, middle England was awakening and beginning to don her first spring garments. The lower branches of the trees were clothed with buds, here and there an open leaf shewed its first delicate green. Upon the banks, and in the hollows the primroses were starring the grass by thousands. Under their own leaves bloomed the sweet-scented bells of the violet; the little white lambs were trotting about in the parks, the snow-drops and the golden crocusses were long ago dead, the air was refreshing and mild as the breath of hope, and the sun shone out joyously over half-clothed wood and springing grass, and gilded the first exquisite green of the tasselled larch, and the birds were twittering, and the little lake was glancing. Thoroughly awake and real was the country side, no hushing snow clothes of winter time, no dreaming moonlight of summer time—all, all was fresh as the first joys of childhood, all was full of the teeming, beautiful, earnest life of spring. And Macnellan, now nearly convalescent, was wheeled out into a sunny part of the park, where the air blew the mildest, and where the primroses clustered thickest.

The gardener's son, a civil lad, in jerkin, stood near ready to move him on to any other place he might choose to name. By him, leaning against the stem of a tree, stood the smiling-faced mesmeriser. Leslie's clothes were of a new cut, he was perfumed with musk, he wore a becoming deer-stalker hat, a handsome gold chain hung from his fob, he held a pair of kid gloves in his hands—his white fat hands; he looked fresh and comfortable, and perfectly easy in mind. Macnellan, yellow and ghastly from illness, worn to a shadow, and ghoul-like in his hideousness, kept those dull, gleaming eyes of his fixed upon the mesmeriser; he hated him, he distrusted him, and so he watched him.

"I am only too glad to see such a favourable change in you, Mr. Macnellan. I am sure you look in charming health this morning."

Leslie was no fool; he was not trying to flatter Macnellan by such a false and ludicrous assertion, but then Leslie did not want to flatter Macnellan; he knew there was nothing to be gained from him, he wanted on the contrary to torment him. Leslie liked tormenting even when he had no particular hatred to the person tormented. Macnellan was caustic and cruel also, but never without a real or supposed cause, and at first he mistook Leslie; he thought the man was a fool, and did want to flatter him.

"Yes," he said, "in charming health; look at this yellow hollow face, look at these talons of fingers, look here at this stump of what was a limb—charming is just the word," and Macnellan gave a snorting laugh of scorn.

"In a short time you will be able to go about on a crutch."

Something like colour came into the

withered cheek of the invalid, he raised his hand, forgot himself in his wrath, and swore a fearful oath, that he would never exhibit his maimed and crippled body in that manner.

"I will henceforth sit," he said, in a voice choking with rage, for he could read the cold, satirical gleam in the other's eye. "I will sit henceforth and be drawn about by paid fellows, who will bear my tempers, and be the slaves of my caprice. There are plenty who would come to me in hopes of finding a place in my will—what spree to disappoint them, eh?"

"Quite in unison with that benevolent disposition of yours, Mr. Macnellan," said Leslie, in the sweetest of voices, and with the most honeyed of smiles, and he took off his cap to Macnellan, in deep, mock respect.

"Why, confound you, sir!" said Macnellan, "what do you mean? Why do you choose me out as a target for your wit? Do you want a cheque in payment for the devil's tricks you have practised upon me?"

Macnellan was as shrewd as Leslie, only that his mind was rather weakened by illness and suffering, and his irritable nerves did not leave him so much self-command as formerly, but he was beginning to attack the other now, as we shall see.

Leslie's face brightened at the mention of a cheque; he had refused payment from Thorpe, for a reason of his own, and because he had wished to appear as a gentleman in his eyes, but now a cheque from this rich and furious old sinner would be a different thing; besides, he was going with all his family to the continent, the very next day, and it did not much matter now what Alton thought of him, he never meant to see it again. A cheque would be useful, if only for travelling expenses; he thought of this, and his face lost its mocking leer.

"I have had a great deal more to do with your recovery than ever Doctor Molson had."

"Do you want a cheque?"

"I am going to Paris to-morrow, and with a family travelling expenses are high."

"Do you want a cheque?"

"I leave it to your generosity to decide that. I leave it rather to your sense of honour and honesty."

"Then you *do* want a cheque?"

"It would be acceptable, sir, certainly."

"Then go without it; ha! ha! ha! did you think I was fool enough to mean it? I *may* stand in need of a crutch, but while I have my senses, I shall know how to take better care of my money than to trust it in your keeping. If I had meant to give you anything, I should have done it weeks ago, when you were fawning and flattering me, up stairs. You must find some other way to get to the continent."

Leslie's lip grew livid with pent-up rage, and Macnellan hardly liked the look he cast upon him.

"Here, Jem," said he to the youth who

was standing at some distance, "wheel me down round there to that clump of elms. Can you manage the wheel on the grass?"

Leslie walked off; the next day his family accompanied him to Paris.

* * * *

"I want to pay your bill, Doctor," said Macnellan, that same afternoon, when, driven in by the April rain, and a coy, chilling wind, he sat discussing mulled port and toasted biscuits by the fire in his room, "I want to pay your bill, Doctor Molson; is it a heavy one?"

The good physician, whose skill had, under Providence, saved the rich patient, and who was himself a very wealthy man, with no children, gave a noble answer to Macnellan's query.

"Your bill to me is more than a hundred pounds; pay it instead to St. Jude's Hospital."

"Why, confound it," said Macnellan, with

a puzzled look, "what good does that do you?"

"A great deal; I have no children, so I am always saving and begging for my poor patients in St. Jude's. I am a St. Jude's man, you know, born under the shadow of the Cathedral."

"Then you set up for a good man, do you, Doctor Molson?" said Macnellan, with a caustic smile.

The good Doctor reddened, and then he said bluntly:—

"Well, sir, nobody can say I am a bad one, I try to do my duty as far as I can. I hate humbug. Well, yes, I suppose I do set up for a good man. I never thought of it in that way, though. I have been a very lucky fellow—I have got on well. I don't want your hundred pounds, except for the Hospital."

"And will it be put in the papers?" said Macnellan, sneering. "Will all St. Jude's know that the Doctor gave up the hundred pounds? Bah! (feeling in his pocket) what a humbug this world is! You did just the same when you wore a pinafore, and gave up your cake to your little sister; everybody said 'What a good boy,' and you felt good all over. Well, there's the pocket cheque book, one hundred pounds, will that do?"

The Doctor took the cheque quietly, like a man and a gentleman; he thanked his cynical patient, and went home contented.

* * * *

There are two facts connected with the burglary which I forgot to state; one is that Crib, the faithful watch-dog, had in the morning been found stiff and poisoned. The other is, that Mostyn had been examined at the trial, but nothing had been proved against him; he was afterwards dismissed.

CHAPTER XVI.

TEMPTATION.

The next day Macnellan was wheeled into the library, and then he and Mr. Thorpe had an interview, in which all the victory was on the side of the crippled Crœsus.

"I was willing to marry your girl at one time, Thorpe, now I am not willing; marriage in my state would be a mockery, so you must be kind enough to cash up as soon as possible."

He waved the one yellow claw that remained to him towards Thorpe as he spoke.

"I must try and get what good I can out

of life," he continued. "I am henceforth an incumbrance to whoever is with me, except for the money I can leave or pay; money is the only good that remains to me, and I must take care of it. I suppose you can find the whole sum by next week."

"I have only eighty thousand pounds in the funds," said Thorpe in a low tone.

"You have this house and these grounds you can mortgage them for the rest."

"I must sell them," said Thorpe, sulkily.

"You must do what you please," said Macnellan, "only you must pay me; and you can deduct two hundred pounds for any expense I may have put you to."

"By the way, what about the Dividends? *that* must be paid; I recommended you to the Mining Company—so that, I must have seen to, if you please."

"I can't help thinking you very hard altogether, to drive me into a corner like this," blurted out Thorpe; "you might let me pay some by instalments, and wait for the rest; you really take a pleasure in my ruin."

"Well," said Macnellan, "you know Rochefoucauld's oft-quoted remark, that we take a pleasure in the misfortunes of our friends,—such is human nature."

"Such," said Mr. Thorpe, "is *fiendish* nature."

"Perhaps you think me more akin to the devil's than the human species? I was cursed with an ugliness, to which I trace all my misfortunes and faults, and I believe, Thorpe, that if I had possessed your thin nostril, and clear complexion, and tall, fine figure, I should have been a good man—perhaps as good as you are."

"I don't pretend to be good, and you know that well!"

"You certainly have not anything very angelic in your eyes at this moment, but I suppose you can't help that! Wouldn't it have been a good thing for you if I had died, eh?"

It was a dangerous question to put to Thorpe at that moment, had Macnellan but known it; his light eyes flashed upon the maimed man, anxiously.

"I wonder," pursued Macnellan, daringly, "I wonder you and that soft villain, the mesmeriser, did not conspire to cook some hellish mess, when I was at my worst, and put me out of your way. Didn't the thought strike you, or did your courage fail?"

Thorpe laughed harshly.

"Macnellan, you talk like an idiot;" but his voice shook as he spoke, and he opened the window soon after, remarking, "this room is hot."

"I'll go now, please," said Macnellan, "if you'll ring the bell; I want to get back to my room, my head aches a little."

He was taken back to his room, and Thorpe still stood by the open window, inhaling the fresh breeze, and looking towards the far country; the whispers of spring brought no peace to the man who dreaded less than a thousand a year and Kidderminster carpets; he began to wish more vehemently than ever that Macnellan had died, he even began to regret.——

* * * *

That evening he dined with his wife in the library; as they were alone, and they sat over their dessert late, he began to talk to her, he went very far, he even *reproached* her with her cowardice; if she had helped him, he ventured to say, they would not have been obliged to give up their property now. She sat and listened for some time without answering.

"My diamonds," she said, at last; "what a frightful loss they were to me—I wonder if they will ever be traced?"

"Why the devil do you fly from the subject?"

"Because nothing can come of discussing it. Of course Macnellan is implacable; we must go abroad, as I said before."

"I'll be hanged first!" when the words were out he turned white, and cowered over the fire. "Maria, I could kill him by next week, and no trace;" he spoke in a whisper, but she motioned him to silence. He went on—"A safe, a certain means, as though he had died in a fit; an animal poison, a secret of science worth learning; but if I told you of it you might betray me. Listen: I prick his hand accidentally, *quite* accidentally, in passing; in a week he is dead! then throw open the house, and let all the faculty come and examine him. I tell you there would be no trace."

"Your own nervousness would betray you, if nothing else. I tell you it never could be done," and they talked on for hours; the only arguments the lady used against the deed were on the score of its risk and danger. She never once asked her husband how he could do this great wickedness, and sin against God? Six months before she might have done this, but lately the death of

Macnellan had been so ardently desired, both by her husband and self, that she had come to look upon him as an evil beast, whom it would be well to put out of the way if possible; but she was far too prudent to embark in such an enterprise, and at last Thorpe declared he would do it unassisted.

"He is a wretch," he said, "who deserves hanging, if you knew half his bad actions, Mrs. Thorpe."

Mrs. Thorpe coldly said she did not doubt that; and at length the household retired for the night, and both the Thorpes slept well.

The next morning, as they sat at breakfast, a letter was handed to Mrs. Thorpe. She broke the seal, and read it through without speaking, but Mr. Thorpe noticed that her eyes glistened and her cheeks glowed as she read; she tossed the letter to him, and said, triumphantly,

"Now, all is right!"

"Have you heard of your diamonds?"

He took the letter up and began to read it, at first carelessly, but his eyes shone before he got to the bottom of the first page. The letter was from the lawyer of her rich nabob uncle, who had quarrelled with her in her youth, but in a sudden freak he had left her three hundred thousand pounds—one hundred thousand settled upon her daughter Ella, the rest to descend to her son at her death. Here was wealth and honour for the Thorpes. Ella, too, was an undoubted heiress, and might yet marry an Earl. Let them sell out of the funds, and sell Alton too—it had not been a prosperous home to them; let them pay that wretched old sinner upstairs, and their other debts; and then let them go to London and buy some sweet place at Richmond, carry with them their treasures of paintings and Dresden, and furniture, and then live like princes on the wife's large income. Arthur could do as he liked about purchasing an estate when he came of age. And all was prosperity and affluence. Away with the thoughts of dark deeds and Kidderminster carpets! Soon should lovely Ella's wedding bells ring, when she was led to the altar by a nobleman!!

Unfeigned congratulations from Macnellan (so he said at least) were theirs. They gave him ample security for his debt, and they set about the selling of Alton; and soon after this Macnellan hired a servant and another attendant and went to London, where he occupied some splendid apartments in Pall Mall; and then Ella wrote to beg that she might come home, if only for a week, that she might take one more look at the dear old place, so she said. And Ella came down, *not* looking so sprightly as might have been expected under the circumstances.

"You are now a greater heiress, Ella, than Miss Elliot," said her mother. "You must be *very careful* who you marry."

Ella walked rapidly out upon the balcony, and essayed to smell at some spring creeper which clustered there.

"How is poor Kate Hall, mamma?" she said at last.

"Oh! poor thing, dying, no doubt of it, so Doctor Molson says."

"What lovely weather it is," said Ella, "I shall go and see her," and she descended to the garden, and took her way towards the park keeper's cottage. Ella's eyes were tender and tearful, as she wound along towards the cottage. She looked down at the springing grass, and sighed a little. She had uttered no slang since her return to Alton. This day was Sunday, and the Easter Bells set up a joyous peal, at which sound she started.

CHAPTER XVII.

THE EASTER BELLS.

KATE HALL lay back upon a sofa in the tiny parlour amid a heap of white pillows; when Ella saw the thin changed face with the unmistakable *something* in its expression, at which most of us have trembled at some time—she paused by the threshold of the door, and her heart seemed to stand still. There was the gold brown hair bound round the head in close braids, the great bright eyes were fixed upon her; the worn shadowy hand was extended to bid her welcome, and a smile was upon the mouth, sad, but not sorrowful.

"Miss Ella, when did you come back?"

"Last night—Oh! Kate! Kate, what have they done to you, to bring you to this—you were well when I left?"

"Sit down dear, there. No, I was not well, I was not well last autumn. This has been coming on some time;" and here the cruel cough impeded her utterance. She put her handkerchief to her lips, and drew it away stained with red blood of her young life.

Ella turned deadly pale, and threw up the little window. She breathed the air of the fresh morning, laden with the delicate perfume of the spring flowers, and through the fields came wafted the joyous sound of the Easter Bells.

"Are you going to church, dear Ella?"

"Oh, no, I am come to stay with you all the time," she returned, and held the thin hand in hers.

"Kate, dear, I was often unkind to you;" a choking sob finished the sentence for Ella.

"Oh, no," said Kate, "you were petulant

sometimes; but, Ella, if my death can make you think seriously, and turn to the sure rock of defence, how glad am I to lay down my poor useless life."

"Useless, no, Kate, mine is a useless life—mine the selfish life of pleasure—of heartless gaiety. You can lie there and fancy you hear the music of heaven; but if I were to come to my death, how I should tremble at the thought of my wasted past."

"Waste it no longer, beautiful Ella; with your health, and gifts, and wealth, what a useful labourer you might become in Christ's vineyard." She used those metaphors which the Bible teaches, and which are so often upon the lips of the canting, and hard sort of religionists, that they lose their pathos, their deep mystical beauty, and become but idle words in the ears of many of us.

"I am afraid I can never be a good person," said Ella, "Mr. Yardly has spoiled me for religion."

"Because one man makes the mistake of

judging, and punishing too harshly, it is wrong to distrust a religion, a church, almost a God," said Kate.

"But, Kate, to leave that subject, the world is meant to be very pleasant, and life is intended to be positively sweet, I am quite sure of it, only something always happens to mar one's happiness; we have the full capacities for enjoyment, and then the delight is snatched from us; it would be so easy to be good if one were happy."

The large lustrous eyes were full of meaning.

"Ella, is it you I hear talking in that way? Have you not everything to make you happy?—wealth, health?"

"But because you, Kate, have always been denied those boons, do you make them the staple commodity of happiness? there is something infinitely sweeter than those, but, poor Kate, you have been refused all. *Yours has* been a sad, striving, tasteless, empty life, and yet you could have enjoyed, had you possessed; you must have had longings for home, for friends—for love," she added, in a lower tone, "and all this has been denied you, and you are called upon to die a lingering, painful death in your youth."

And Kate answered her in the words of the great founder of our religion:

"The cup which my Father has given me, shall I not drink it?"

"Kate, are you happy?"

"Oh, so happy! I would not stand where you do now, Ella, not to be endowed with your wealth, your health, your beauty, your capacities for usefulness and happiness."

"Then, Kate, you have no regret in leaving this world; there is no face it would give you pleasure to see by your bedside, no hand you would care to clasp in a last farewell? Is there no one you would like me to summon—your brother?"

"I do not know where he is," said Kate, and the bright hectic dyed her cheeks. "I shall leave my Bible to you, to send him; if you should ever hear of his place of abode, you will do that?"

"Oh, yes, Kate. But is there no one *else*?"

"Who?" said Kate, while a slight shade of something like displeasure flitted across her brow.

"Kate, don't be angry with me." Ella bent down her head and whispered, "Mr. Cruize, I thought you loved him."

"Oh!" said Kate, in a tone with just a tinge of faint surprise in it, "what put that into your head?"

"It was true," said Ella, resolutely, "you did."

"I was weak, and fond, and vain, dear Ella, as many other women have been before and since; but why do you bring up that old tale now, it seems to me so very long ago since I crushed that weakness?"

"Is it crushed?"

"Quite."

"Then you don't want to see him, it would give you no pleasure?"

"None at all, it would be indecorous besides."

"Bother indecorous," said Ella, impatiently. "Oh, Kate, I want to tell you something."

"What, dear?"

Then Ella bent down and whispered a long time into the ear of Kate; when she raised her face again it was pale with emotion, and Kate's was scarcely less so:

"May God watch over you, Ella," she said, "and keep you from harm. You need great care. I will pray for you, that you may be kept out of temptation."

"You will not tell?"

"No, and yet what an additional safeguard it would be if this were known. Now you will be beset with temptations on all hands. Oh, Ella, will you pray sometimes? will you read the book of life? will you leave off mocking at good things?"

"Here," said Ella, "let me mix you some of this lemon drink, and wouldn't you like your fire stirred up a little?"

Afterwards Ella read some of the gospel according to St. John aloud to Kate, and then she knelt down and read some prayers aloud from a little book. Soon after, the Easter bells struck up again joyously, the people were coming out of church, and presently there came a gentle tap at the door of the cottage, and Mr. Clyne, the curate, walked in. Ella began to put on her hat and gloves, and seemed in a great hurry to go.

"Don't go away on my account, Miss Thorpe," said the Curate.

"Well, to tell you the truth, Mr. Clyne, we have been reading the Bible and praying a long time, and I think enough is better than too much, even of a good thing. I shouldn't attend a bit if you prayed the best prayer that ever was prayed." She spoke in her old wicked, reckless manner.

"I am not going to pray," said Mr. Clyne.

"Do, do stop!" entreated Catherine.

So Ella stopped. The curate had brought oranges in his pocket for Kate.

"I shall make you some nice jelly to-night," said Ella.

Kate replied, "Thank you," and then turned to Mr. Clyne.

"Mr. Clyne, do you think it is meant for man to be happy on this earth?" she asked; "or is this world only a place of labour and sorrow? do tell me what you believe."

Kate was of the same way of thinking in the matter of religion as the Rev. F. Yardly; she was of the staunchest evangelical school. She believed in the lake of fire, in the uselessness of personal effort in the method of salvation, in the election of the few. The curate's wider and more peculiar views did not meet her own, and she would have chosen the Rev. F. Yardly in preference; though not so amiable and perfect as a man, he was, she considered, more qualified as a teacher. But the Rev. Yardly came seldom near her, whereas the pious curate never forgot her bedside; he came, too, full of the hope and spirit of the gospel, and lately Kate had taken more pleasure in his conversation, and now she asked him what he thought of happiness below.

"The human cup is so mixed," he said, "that it is sometimes difficult to distinguish the bitter from the sweet, but I believe that those who drain the bitterest dregs suffer somehow through the wrongs which their fellow creatures bring upon them in some indirect way. God has, for some purpose, let the human skein of affairs become so tangled that it would take a century to unravel it. I believe man is expected to do it himself, to regenerate his race, to right its wrongs, to bind up the brŏken in heart, to teach the ignorant; and in time this will come about. I verily believe progress is marching on, progress towards right; in another century and a half there shall be no starving, no gaols, no thieves, no murderers; all men shall be enlightened, free and equal, all shall worship one God and acknowledge one Saviour, all shall vie with each other in deeds of heroism, of self-devotion, of kindness, of charity—all this is coming about, the time when there shall be no more slaves, no more sins, no more sufferings!"

"Now," thought Ella, "I see why they call him the mad curate." Then she spoke:

"But, Mr. Clyne, while your century and a half of progress is marching on, people are dying, and suffering, and sinning around us. People are hating each other, and filling the world with wrath, and anger, and clamour. Now we won't talk about what the world will be when your hundred and fifty years are over, we won't talk about the smouldering spirit of right preparing to burst forth from under the hideous chaos of wrong which lies over it, because when that great light comes to brighten all the world, and consume all grievances, we—you and I—will have lain some years silent in our coffins; and not only that, but we shall have crumbled into charnel dust, and perhaps sprung up again, according to the materialistic and chemical view of the subject, in the form of grasses and herbs.

Kate, don't look so distressed, you know what a rattle brain I am. Well, Mr. Clyne, what we want to know is whether you think we—*we* living, breathing, eating, drinking creatures of to-day are expected to find happiness in this life, or only to look upon this world as a vale of tears, a school of labour, where duty and virtue are the only means of happiness, where we must in short practice self-denial, and look for our reward in Heaven alone? Now answer that. We know well what Brimstone Yardly thinks, I have just given his opinion; now tell us what you think about it."

"Some," said Mr. Clyne, "many, alas! are so placed that it is impossible for them to find the sweets of the earth, those good and pleasant gifts which it was God's will at first that all his creatures should enjoy. Countless numbers spend all their lives, good and virtuous lives, many of them in privations, loneliness, unpitied trials, unmitigated sufferings. To them this life can offer nothing good, not because the All Merciful would deny them happiness, but because this world is so organised, or disorganised by circumstances, the time is so 'out of joint,' that it becomes inevitable that many should bear the burden and heat of the day, while others sit idle in the market-place. But to some it is given all things richly to enjoy; to those I would say, 'live your life, your full, happy human life which God has blessed you with; love and be loved, plant vineyards and sit under your own fig trees, and bless the King of Heaven, for His mercy endureth for ever!'"

Kate's cough was troublesome for a little while, but when she spoke again, it was with earnestness—

"Then, Mr. Clyne, what comfort do you hold out to those whose lives are bare, and empty, and, so far as this world is concerned, desolate?

"I would say in the words of *Him* whose cause I serve, 'rejoice and be exceeding glad, for great is your reward in Heaven.'"

Kate smiled brightly.

"That is the sweetest of all rewards, is it not, Mr. Clyne?

"Then," said Ella, I suppose you think me one of the fig tree parties, because I've come into a lot of money, Mr. Clyne, eh?"

"Are you not then?" said the curate, but he did not smile at the madcap's attempt at wit.

"No, I have a skeleton in my cupboard. 'A death's head at the wine,'" she spoke in a sad tone; "my life is far less painted 'with the hues of promise' than you might think."

"I can give no advice, when I know so little," said the curate.

"I only wanted your opinion upon human happiness, and I've got it. I did not ask for advice, dear curate. It may be summed up into few words. Now all is going on any how, everything is out of order; some get figs, and some get thistles; those who get figs are to eat them and be thankful, those who get thistles are to do the best they can and look for reward in Heaven. But in another hundred and odd years thistles will be at a discount, everybody will be eating figs, and sharing them with his neighbours. In fact," she added, rising to go, "everybody will be as good a saint as the Rev. Robert Clyne. Don't fancy I'm chaffing you. I know how good you are, and how true, and patient, and unselfish; there, I must not say all I think, for if so, you will think me a humbug. Good-bye now, Mr. Clyne. By the way, do you know what has become of your protegé, the schoolmaster of Alton, where is he?"

"I have no idea, Miss Thorpe; he has not written to me for some time, and my last letter to him was returned through the dead letter office."

"What a sell! Kate, good-bye," she bent down, and kissed the pale forehead, and she dropped a bright tear upon the face. "Kate, good-bye," and she walked out into the air just as the last sound of the Easter Bells was dying away.

CHAPTER XVIII.

SPRING BLOSSOMS.

While the spring grew and increased in beauty day by day, Kate Hall's life waned gradually away; the cough grew weaker, the cheek whiter, the breathing more laboured. Ella pertinaciously refused to leave Alton while her companion lay dying; she spent whole days with the invalid in the little close parlour, and Mrs. Thorpe warned her of the danger of infection, but Ella recklessly persisted in attending to the sick girl; she became far less joyous, and thoughtless than formerly, but she was queer as ever, still using slang on occasions, even with tears in her eyes, and tender sorrow at her heart. She used to read the Bible a great deal to Kate; she used to wonder at the firmness of her faith and trust; she used to bring out odd startling things suddenly, sometimes, and she used to talk irreverently now and then of the mysteries of life and death, and eternity; not that she blasphemed or mocked, but the organ of veneration was so little developed that she scarcely understood the difference between things sacred and profane. And she felt Kate's dying deeply; the inevitable, inexorable decree that had gone forth seemed to her cruel.

"Oh, Kate, how happy I would have tried to make you, if you might have been spared, and yet I did not care much for making you happy when I thought you were well, but I am changed since then." And the madcap wept.

"You were my first friend, you were always kind to me; it was only want of thought that made you rough," gasped Kate, feebly.

"Kate, I only think too much now; I lie awake and cry, and moan sometimes, when I reflect on the foolish, wicked things I have done, and I am not like you. I was not framed for renunciation. I cannot forego."

"But you must," said Kate solemnly.

"Oh, to you it was easy; but to me—all self-will, fire, impatience—it is madness."

"Ella, you will not look for help where help may be found."

"Kate, dear, that sweet spirit of resignation which you preach, and meekly practise, has never been given to me. I'm in the very gall of bitterness," as old Yardly would say.

"I pray that you may be brought to the truth," said Kate. She was silent a little, and then went on again. "I believe you will. I have been brought up all my life, Ella, to look forward to this change, which is now coming, as my supremest joy: when I was very young I read no poems, and works of fiction, as you have done; my ideas of the beautiful were what I could draw from the glorious descriptions of the Scriptures, the New Jerusalem descending from Heaven out of God, the golden streets, the great white throne, the sea of glass mingled with fire; all these beautiful realities have grown dearer to me year by year; and now I go to them, to that Lamb of God who is the light of the city, to that One who sitteth upon the throne, judging righteously."

"And, Kate, you who believe so much, do you never feel nervous?"

"Never; you know what He says, 'He that believeth in me I will in no wise cast out.' I have believed all my life He will lift me in his arms, and carry me in his bosom, when I pass out of this poor, weak, shrinking house of flesh."

Ella sobbed convulsively, and clung to Kate's hand.

"Kate, I am not shedding these tears for you, they are for myself. You are going fast and safe to happiness. I am thinking of my wretched, faithless self; and Kate, not one soul on earth to love me, I feel it now—not even mamma. I do feel it now; cold, she is cold as ice! And I must never think of that, I must never have a loving husband nor little children."

"And I have had no one to love me," said Kate, "no one on earth, that is; but in Heaven I have always had a loving father. He will be yours too, Ella."

"Ah, but I want some human love," moaned Ella; "I do indeed."

Soon after that the dying patient and the beautiful heiress parted, and Ella went home in the sad light of the spring evening. The dew was heavy on the grass, the shadows were creeping over the trees, and a chilly wind sprung up, and caused her to draw her mantle more closely round her. When she entered the house the servant was carrying up the tea-things; she flung her hat on the table in the hall, and rushed as she was, with swollen eyes and pale face, into the drawing-room.

"Ella, how you do disfigure yourself with

crying, and shutting yourself up in that close room, with poor Miss What's-her-name. You will ruin your complexion, and in another week I want you to be in London, looking pretty, and going to the balls. You know I have taken a grand furnished house for the season."

"I did not know it."

"And I mean to have this furniture and the pictures stowed in St. Jude's until we decide on a new house."

"Oh!"

"You don't seem to take the least interest, Ella, in anything. I'm sure you ought to be thankful and contented; you are a most fortunate girl, and not wear your life away because poor Miss What's-her-name happens to be dying; it can't be helped, you know. She has always had the seeds of consumption in her."

"Yes, mamma, but one cannot help having some feeling; one has a human heart, after all." And she sighed.

"Of course," said Mrs. Thorpe, "I should very sorry if you had no feeling—is that too much sugar for you?—but when people begin to fret about what is inevitable, and not their own relations either, it becomes too much to bear—try that muffin. Don't you fancy the cook puts too much butter?"

"Why shouldn't I fret if I like?"

"It makes you look plainer and older."

"Why can't I make myself look ugly if I choose?"

"You will not choose among the London belles. You will want to vie with them. Now you will have loads of offers. Challoner will come and open his great blue eyes again. I do hope, Ella, you will have nothing to do with him."

"Don't fear."

"Or with anybody else as poor and absurd as he is; you have had your little romance, now look for reality."

"What is reality?" said Ella, with a curious expression, screwing up her eyes: "poor Kate would tell me there was no reality on earth, all earthly joys are fading commodities, Heaven alone is real. Now what do you think?"

"Of course, I mean position; your father has been a merchant, now our wealth will bring us into higher society. Why should you think of law students, or poor lieutenants? Why should you not marry a nobleman or a first-class Member of Parliament?"

"Ah, why not?"

"You speak mockingly, which is undutiful. If all poor Miss Hall's religion does not teach you to respect your mother, I would not give much for it."

"She is always preaching to me about duty to you."

"I am glad to hear it; did you take her the jelly?"

"Yes; but she can't swallow now."

"Poor thing!"

The next morning, while Ella was dressing, there came a solemn sound across the green corn lands towards the village; she started and turned white; it came again that dull, awful sound! What a spirit seems in the mouth of a bell at such a moment!—what a dull crushing weight falls upon the human heart! "Gone," it says, "for ever from among men; gone to that mysterious country from which NONE ever return; gone—and though you laid down your own life as the price, you could never drain one word more from those cold lips, one answering gleam from that filmy eye."

"It's for poor Miss Hall," said Fanny, "she died this morning at four o'clock."

When, on the afternoon of the next day, Ella entered that tiny parlour at the lodge keeper's, there were several village women there, and among them Mrs. King, Martin's landlady. She was a Londoner, and she considered herself superior to all the village. The women dropped low curtseys when Miss Thorpe came in, and took the white cloth off that long narrow case, and then the lid, and there lay the shrouded form, with spring blossoms on the breast, and face so fair, so calm, such an awful smile upon the lips, as though she had indeed gazed upon the hidden mysteries of God! How changed that face was, and yet how like! Had those lips really spoken to Ella? how long ago that *must* have been. "Now she is as old as death."

Ella burst into hysterical weeping.

"She went very easy, poor thing," said the lodge-keeper's wife, looking at the stirless figure. "I was with her, and Mr. Clyne. The doctor hadn't been gone ten minutes. She was as 'appy as if she'd a been going home."

"When my Anna went," said Mrs. King, she says to me, 'Mother,' she says, 'I'm a going 'ome,' she says."

Poor Mrs. King, virago and gossip, had still that human heart when she spoke of her dead Anna; tears gathered in her eyes and fell into her apron.

Ella went home, looking and feeling ill.

A few days afterwards she stood by the grave, and heard the earth fall upon the wooden case, and the solemn words, "Earth to earth, dust to dust," were uttered by the Curate. Kate Hall was buried out of her sight, but she dwelt in her mind always. Ella never forgot the life of patient toil, disappointed love, and joyless striving which had been quenched in its blossom, but which was gone into another and happier sphere—to that home where the weary are at rest.

CHAPTER XIX.

A LITTLE ABOUT THE BALL AT SIR WILLIAM BIGOTT'S.

Two months later, at a gay and brilliant ball given by Sir William Bigott, a man high in the law, Ella Thorpe, the great heiress, was the decided belle of the room. She was dressed in a ball costume of faint pink, a rich silk skirt, and white misty lace over it, a tiara of white camelias in her raven hair, and she wore a set of rubies which her mother had purchased for her. She certainly was radiantly lovely that night; roses mantling on her dark cheeks, her wonderful lustrous eyes gleaming, and darkening, and brightening; and she waltzed to perfection—she seemed to float round the room, supported by that idolized "Lancer." The regiment stationed at Hampton Court had been invited and was present, and it was with one of those irresistible members of society, an "officer" who had seen service, who was the fashion, nay the rage, that Ella was flirting horribly, if flirting horribly consists in dancing seven times running with one man, in listening to all he says, and saying a great deal herself. Major Super was a man of twenty-eight, promoted thus early for his heroism in India. Major Super had merry blue-grey eyes and a fresh complexion, and dark brown hair; he was neither tall nor short, nor stout nor thin, nor ugly nor handsome, nor gifted nor stupid, but he was Major Super *par excellence*; his family was very good, and he had a tolerable private fortune. Marriage was not in his line unless he could bag an heiress without trouble, love was not in his line, enthusiasm was not in his line ; in short, it is surprising to find how little was in his line, and how such a "love of an officer" was best described by negatives. Major Super's manner was marked by that dignified and elegant carelessness which usually distinguishes gentlemen in the Army; —he was not the least deferential to ladies, some would have called him rude; he openly stated that he was in debt, and seemed rather proud of that great fact, as were most of his brother officers. (In a lower rank, the man who is in debt for necessaries is covered with contumely, but the world, with that even-handed justice for which it is remarkable, glorifies the gay insolvent officer who is in debt for useless and absurd superfluities, so that a regiment goes boasting of its debts, and the ladies laugh, and call the dear creatures all the finer fellows for it.) Major Super used to approach any young lady known to him by name, and who was on terms of slight intimacy with him, and he did not request the pleasure, nor beg the honour, as was once the old fashion, but he would quietly articulate three words, "Dance with me," and then having thus commanded the young lady, for the words were not put in the form of a question, Major Super would lead her off by the hand, and condescend to dance with her until he was quite tired. And now he had got Ella, or rather Ella had got him; he admired her, as he admitted afterwards, and said she was a clever girl.

"I suppose you like balls very much, don't you?" said Ella, when they were sitting down to rest.

"Oh, I like them well enough when I can get hold of a good partner," said Major Super. "Some ladies are such insufferable weights, like lead, enough to make a man's arm ache for three days after," and the Major yawned at the heavy recollection.

"I hope you don't mean me?"

"No! if I had I should not have asked you to dance a second time; you dance beautifully!"

"How kind you are to say so. Who do you think the prettiest girl in the room?"

"You!"

"I knew you could not help saying that; but leaving me out of the question?"

"I could not possibly leave you out of the question!"

"Don't you think that Miss Wyatt pretty?"

"Where is she?"

"There, sitting opposite, with that black moustached—"

"Ah!" and Super put his eye glass in his eye, and indulged in a long stare.

"Yes, she is pretty," said he.

"Such a fair complexion, and such perfect features."

"I don't care anything about complexion."

"Don't you?"

"I hardly know if a young lady is fair, or red, or brown, or what she is."

"How nice for the muddy and sallow faced ones, not to be quizzed."

"They may get quizzed for all that."

"No doubt. I suspect you are an awful quiz."

"Why should you think that?"

"You have the look about you."

"What is the look?"

"Oh, it is not to be described; but it's there."

"Well, I am very sorry it's there."

Then this erudite and soul stirring conversation came to a stop; for a short time the Major had nothing to say and Ella was gathering up her forces to attack him; she had treated him to flattery, and he was lazingly basking in her smile. Now she was going to be pert and waspish.

"Do you like riding?" she said, suddenly.

"I like it well enough in good weather, and on a good road."

"Do you like to ride in the park?"

"Sometimes; it's rather fun."

"I suppose you spend a good deal of time in reading?"

"No; why should you suppose that?"

"Why, people who live their lives very earnestly, enjoy themselves very much, and take a great interest in what goes on around them, seldom care to read much. I'm one of that sort; but *you* seem half alive over everything, so I concluded you were a great reader, perhaps a poet, or a dreamer."

"I am not then, either the one or the other—I like to take things easily—I can't find out the pleasure of exciting oneself about things; there's nothing worth getting up early for that I can see."

"But you got excited in India, when you stormed Delhi?"

Now the Major did not like to talk about Delhi; he was a gentleman, and he was brave, and he was not a boaster, except in the matter of his debts, and there, perhaps, society was more to blame than he was, so he turned the subject of his warlike deeds by criticising the dress of an elderly lady who passed; he declared her head looked like a stewpan.

"I don't care about stewpans," said Ella; "let the old party dress as she likes. I shouldn't wonder if she does not come down a regular cropper, if she tries to cross the room while those people are *knocking* about in that waltz."

"*Knox* has always been opposed to dancing since the days of Mary of Scotland," said a voice at Ella's elbow. She turned and saw young Mr. Rollins, the facetious friend of Challoner, whom she had not spoken to or seen since the autumn of the last year. Of course they shook hands and were very friendly, and Ella saw that the "Super" and the wit were acquainted.

"I came to solicit the honour of your hand for this quadrille?"

"Oh! only for the quadrille; I thought it might have been a public proposal;" the soldier opened his eyes. "That's right, Major Super—I shall bring you up to a pitch of excitement by my oddities before I have done. Now I'm going to dance with Mr. Rollins. You can sit here, you like watching well enough? it's nice sleepy work, isn't it?"

"I shall go down and smoke," said the Major. "I don't want to watch you!" he added, candidly.

"Don't you? I flattered myself I had made an indelible impression on—" and she paused.

"My heart!"

"Oh no, you are not burdened with such a thing; your arm, yes, your arm, like those heavy weights you know you were telling me of."

"That would not be indelible," said the Major, literally, and a little pettishly; then Ella went off in the quadrille with Rollins.

"What was this dreadful tale I heard about Alton Hall being robbed? were you there?"

"No, I was here in town."

"What a very odd thing it was; and Mrs. Thorpe did not recover her diamonds?"

"No; it was rather a plague; I should have had them, you know."

"Did you put a clever detective on the scent?"

"Yes; he's scenting away after them now even, and he fancies we shall be able to find them."

"I am sure I hope he may. And there was Miss Hall—did I not read of her behaving most valorously: going down to the plate chest, and brandishing a poker?"

"She is dead," said Ella, in a low tone.

"Dead! nonsense, Miss Thorpe—I know you of old."

"She died," said Ella, "two months ago; pray talk of something else!"

The elegant laughing and flirting groups, the merry dance music, the brilliant room seemed to jar upon Ella's senses when she recalled the narrow box, the white cloth, the changed face, the lowly grave, amid this careless, heartless prodigal life. Rollins' words had conjured up the "death's head at the wine." A few years, and each and everyone of the dancing, quizzing, chattering assembly should lie as stiff, and cold, and changed, and solitary as Kate Hall. She went no further than the grave clothes, and the cold forehead; she had scarcely a true belief in the immortality of the spirit, she was not much given to speculating upon its probable state, she only thought of death as an annihilation; she grew grave and silent. Rollins tried to rouse her.

"What has become of the learned Dominie?" he asked.

Ella was either abstracted or uncourteous, for she did not answer him.

"Miss Thorpe—what has become of your friend, the Dominie; does he still flourish at Alton?"

"He was turned off for getting drunk," said Ella, bluntly.

Rollins was pre-eminently sober, and consequently drunkenness was a vice he was proportionately averse to.

"I had no idea he was a bad character," said Rollins.

"Oh, he was not a bad character—old Brimstone behaved abominably to him."

"Well, not feeling any more drawn with tender chords of love towards the gentleman known as old Brimstone, than you, I must think he was in the right to dismiss a drunkard."

"Dear me! I like a drunkard," said Ella, recklessly.

Rollins laughed.

"Miss Thorpe, I am sorry to find you are not improved since the autumn."

"I like a drunkard," repeated Ella; "a man is not better than a woman if he can't get sprung occasionally."

"I would make you a *bow* if I were in an artificial flower shop instead of a public ball-room."

"What a horrid pun!"

"You know that's my forte."

"Come into the supper-room," said Ella, "and get me an ice!"

"Won't you have a glass of champagne?"

"No, thank you."

"Or fine old whisky, which I have ready for you, Miss Thorpe."

"You have?"

"Yes, in my mind's eye, you know."

"Ah! that's where you used to keep your best stores," so thus chattering they went into the refreshment room, and Ella ate an ice.

"I say, have you heard that I am an heiress now?"

"Yes, I heard it, and I halved the amount you were said to possess; I always believe half of what I hear in every case. If I heard you were married I should fancy you were engaged. If I heard you had built a mansion I should believe it was a cottage. If I heard you had written a novel I should think it was a letter. If I heard you had broken your leg I should fancy it was your finger. If I heard you had eaten a roasted ox I should fancy it was a roasted chicken."

"Well, and how much money do you fancy I have?"

"Well, I forget how much it was I heard you had."

"If you heard I had bought a pair of boots, would you believe that?"

"I should think you had bought one for your left foot."

"If I told you I had a pair of white silk boots on, would you think I had come with one shoe off and one shoe on?—hi diddle diddle dum, my son John!"

"Now, when you know that my name is John, I consider your jibing cruel."

At this moment a slight graceful young man, with fair curly hair, approached the table. Upon his arm leant a beautiful blonde, gorgeously dressed in bright blue silk and pearl ornaments, her magnificent hair, yellow like ripe corn, was dressed in the mode called Eugenie. The girl was Pauline Leslie, the man was Hubert Challoner; Ella knew them both at once. With great self-command she smiled, and extended her hand to the darling.

"What an unexpected pleasure!" she said, with a slight tinge of sarcasm in her tone.

The darling blushed, as was his wont, and extended his hand to meet that of Ella.

Pauline looked as haughty and unconcerned as possible.

"I had no idea that you were here," continued Ella, ignoring Pauline.

"I had no idea that *you* were here," said the darling, recovering his self possession. "Do you not know Miss Leslie? She was a neighbour of yours, Ella."

"I had *not* the pleasure of Miss Leslie's acquaintance," said Ella, very pointedly. "I am only too ravished to make it now. I trust Miss Leslie is in perfect health?"

Miss Leslie thanked Miss Thorpe coldly,

the two beauties contemplated each other with a haughty stare. Lately Mrs. Crane, the farmer's wife, had enlightened Ella a little about the darling's proceedings, so Ella hated Pauline cordially.

"What on earth brings a creature like that to Sir William Bigott's ball?" she thought.

"Are you engaged for the next dance but one?" asked Challoner, not timidly; the darling had too good an opinion of himself ever to be timid.

"No, I will dance it with you with pleasure."

"There, the Mazurka has begun," said Pauline, so she hurried out with Challoner.

"How in the world is that party togged up in that expensive style, and waltzing at Sir William Bigott's ball?" said Ella to Rollins. "She has no right here.

"Who is she?"

"Nobody at all," said Ella, contemptuously.

Rollins laughed.

"She looked solid enough," said he. "Do you mean that she is made of mountain mist, a spirit, something uncanny?"

"I mean that her father was lodging at a farm in Woodly, and was never noticed by a soul; he was in debt up to his ears, and when Macnellan was ill, he used to come to mesmerize him; he is a needy adventurer. I'm certain it is by some mistake that creature is here. I wonder who is her chaperone."

"Let us go, and find out all about it," said Rollins, "a little excitement is refreshing; perhaps we shall find that this 'party' has come under a false name;" and Rollins and Ella went out of the room, and as they went out of hearing, a sort of choking sob sounded from behind the door; and a waiter who, himself concealed, had heard all their colloquy, came out into the room; he wore the borrowed livery of Sir William for the night; his face was ghastly with passion, and his deep set eyes sent out positive gleams of fire; he was gaunt and worn, and his great frame seemed made of bones and skin alone.

"What would she say," he growled, "if she knew her *husband* was here? her husband watching her, and waiting until he has tried every means to raise himself before he claims her; they will all fail, my heart tells me so, but I will possess her before I die. I hate her for her pride; the daughter of an adventurer has no right to dance in the same salon with her, while her husband—great God! am I that proud woman's husband? do I love her still? Not as I did, other feelings will come; she despises me, she would shrink from me, but when I claim her it shall be when her woman's shrieks are beyond the ear of help. I have watched her well; she is heartless; she lets those men jeer her and talk to her with disrespect, while I"—he could not finish his sentence. Poor Martin did not understand how very freely, almost disrespectfully, young gentlemen speak to young ladies in what is termed good society.

The intercourse between Ella and Rollins was innocent of even the shadow of flirtation, and Rollins *did* respect Ella *quite* as much as she deserved, but of this the unhappy schoolmaster knew nothing; trouble, and disappointment, and injustice were fast making him savage, and almost brutal. He said nothing more, and retreated again to the rear.

Meanwhile the unconscious wife was talking to Rollins, and waiting for her turn to dance with the darling. At last it came; Challoner stood up with her in a quadrille or lancers, and then she began:

"Well, I've never forgotten our last interview."

"Have you not?"

"I suppose *you* have?"

"I remember you were in an awful passion."

"I suppose the fair Miss Leslie is never in a passion?"

"I've never seen her in one."

"Are you engaged to her?"

"Engaged," the darling laughed, "there's no chance of my getting engaged for a long time to come."

"How is it *she* is at this ball? You know they were never received at Alton."

"Her father has come into five thousand a year."

"Halve it," said Ella.

"So I am told. They have taken a pretty furnished house in Baker-street, and a German countess who knew them at Wisbaden is patronising Pauline, and has brought her here to night."

"Have you met her before to-night? I mean, lately?"

"Oh, yes, frequently."

"Have you heard of *my* good luck?"

"Yes."

"I have a hundred thousand pounds of my own."

"I am glad to hear it."

"If I had had that at the time of our conversation I should have been Mrs. Challoner now?"

"You would."

"But now," said Ella, "it's different."

"Yes; you would not look at a poor fellow like me now?"

"I am looking at you."

"You would not think of me?"

"I often think of you."

"You would not marry me?"

"That's a different thing."

"You are deserving of some one of importance now," said the darling.

"I'm going to look for a most important man."

"That's right," said Challoner, drily. Ella could not move him an inch.

"I suppose you are desperate about this Pauline?"

"Most desperate," said Challoner, with a

smile. "Don't you see great signs of desperation about me?"

In short, the darling was too many for Ella, and she spent the rest of the evening flirting with the Super Major.

END OF VOL. II.

CPSIA information can be obtained
at www.ICGtesting.com
Printed in the USA
LVHW110810120522
718525LV00003B/59

9 783375 002770